The Legend of Elos Mountain

by

Robert B. Harvey

Layout design by
Sue Finch Photography and Design LLC

ISBN: 9798848037517

Dedication

Bear & Snakey have never let me forget. In the mid 1960s I attended an Indian Pow Wow in Riverside, California. I met an older Indian gentleman who had been born and raised in the Yukon Territory. His name was Clarence Cloudwalker. He claimed to have grown up knowing members of the Tlinket First Nation. His own people were the Kwadacha First Nation. The Kwadacha and the Tlinket tribes both had a long history of being Seagoing and heavily dependent on both Whales and Salmon.

Over the past 50 years I have gathered information and weaved the Legend, that combines two Indian tribes and how they were affected by a Grizzly Bear and a Rattlesnake. There have been a number of people who have played a part in developing this story, beginning with Wanda Meadows, whose roll was pivotal in helping me build the spiritual impact that Bear & Snakey had on, not only the Kiltook people, but on the environment as well as the wild creatures around them. My friend Kevin Wilson gave me invaluable help in crafting the dialogue for both the members of the Kiltook tribe, but also the intricate verbal dance between Bear & Snakey. Last but not least is my sister-in-law Trudine Springer who did a careful copy edit, catching many typos and Donna Menigat for her knowledgeable editing skills.

Introduction

The Legend of Elos Mountain has been 82 years in the writing. I was six-years-old in 1940, when my oldest brother Arnold came home for a visit. We were living in Langlois, about 50 miles south of Coquille, the County Seat of Coos County, Oregon. During that visit, Arnold would take me on his shoulders and we would hike the hills and the Pacific Ocean Coastline that surrounded Langlois, Oregon. My brother told me about Bear & Snakey, two unusual friends, a Grizzly and a Rattlesnake, who he said, lived in a wooden shack that stood high on a hill above the town. I wanted to know how a Grizzly and a Rattlesnake could be friends. My brother explained that they both had been caught in a forest-fire, started unwittingly by an Indian Tribe called the Kiltook people, who lived near the beach at the foot of Elos Mountain. Bear was blind and Snakey had been burned so severely, he could barely crawl.

In order to survive, Bear & Snakey had agreed to work together. Bear was the feet. Snakey, on the other hand, snugly positioned in the dense fur around Bear's neck, was the eyes.

Bear & Snakey sparked an indelible imprint in my imagination, that filled my dreams all the years I was grow-ing up. I joined the Navy in 1951. My first ship was the aircraft carrier, USS Cabot. I began writing articles for the ship's paper, and decided that I must never let "The Legend of Elos Mountain" fade away. I found a book in the Ship's Library that described the coastal Indian tribes in the pacific Northwest. The tribe that grabbed my interest was called the Tlinket tribe, whose home was the Yukon Territory in Northwest British Columbia. I built my imaginary Indian tribe, the Kiltook People around the real-life Tlinket tribe from northwestern Canada. Over the years, I've worked in many different jobs that took over my focus and my energy. No matter how long the diversion, I've always come back to Bear and Snakey.

Table of Contents

The Legend of Elos Mountain

Chapter One
The Kiltook People

Smoke and heat rose into the sky, causing the view of great Elos Mountain to appear and disappear. The peak towered above the small Kiltook Indian village, nestled between the mountain slopes and Elos Bay. A large campfire blazed in the center of the village. Members of the Eagle clan brought a steady flow of red salmon speared from the tribe's fishing platforms. These structures were suspended from cedar logs, sunk vertically into the Kiltook River bank. A total of four cedar platforms extended eight feet over the mouth of the Kiltook River. It entered Elos Bay a quarter of a mile south of the village. Women dried the salmon on large wooden racks, next to the water's edge. The village consisted of 20 wooden lodges. The basic skeleton of each lodge consisted of four permanent vertical poles at the corners, with interconnecting cross members. The roof was made from interwoven planks, held in place by a scattering of heavy rocks. The walls were six foot sections made from smaller poles woven together as removable panels. These panels and the roof planks would be dismantled and transported when the tribe made it's yearly migration to their summer camp.

Fifty feet from shore, a teenage Indian boy, No Face, stood in a small dugout canoe. The tide was beginning to go out and the water was calm. The boy appeared quite handsome with a firm muscular chest, and powerful legs. He balanced carefully on the sides of the canoe and jokingly acted as if he might fall in.

A teenage girl, Morning Star, who was helping the women place fish on the drying racks looked out at No Face. Her long shimmering black hair framed her beautiful face and gorgeous, dark eyes. She looked away, as No Face appeared to fall out of the canoe into the chilly water. The boy dove to the bottom of the bay and used a stone tool to pry an abalone from its rocky perch. Abalone is a large sea snail, prized as food. The beautiful shell is used in making jewelry. Sections of shell are attached to wooden handles and used as carving tools.

No Face grabbed his prize and rose to the surface, dropping the shell into the canoe. He looked up to see if Morning Star was watching. As she bent over the drying rack, Morning Star glanced at No Face, then looked away quickly and focused on the fish she was hanging.

The Shaman of the Kiltook people, Spirit Singer, stood near the water. Around his neck, he wore a necklace with dozens of multi colored feathers. Standing a few feet off the beach, up to his chest in the icy water was another teenage boy, Seemi. He was tall and slim, with dark hollow eyes and a sad expression. He held himself and shivered. Looking at Spirit Singer, Seemi pleaded, "I want to come out now."

Spirit Singer responded impatiently, "They will speak to you, the spirits, and they will tell you when." Listen to their voices."

In a sharp whining voice Seemi said, "I'm freezing. It's cold. I don't hear any Spirits."

"I want to come out now," Seemi pleaded.

Spirit Singer responded angrily, "Stop whimpering and listen." He shook his rattle to call to the spirits and quietly chanted "Great Spirit, give this boy the strength to become a man and to one day proudly wear the circle of feathers that I wear today. Give this boy the wisdom to know what is right. Give this boy…"

Seemi interrupted, saying, "I'm really cold. I think I might pass out."

Spirit Singer dropped the rattle to his side and looked down dejectedly. He shook his head in disgust saying, "Great Spirit, help us."

Seemi feigned a cheerful attitude and said, "I think I hear a spirit."

Inside of you, was there a voice? Spirit Singer asked. "Yes," replied Seemi. "It said I should come out of the water."

Chapter One

Spirit Singer looked at Seemi and said, "Disappointed, that is what you make me."

Seemi blurted out loudly "I tell you I heard the voice."

Spirit Singer responded, "My senses tell me otherwise, but come out if you must."

Seemi leapt from the water and stood shivering on the beach.

Angry with himself Spirit Singer picked up an Alder bough and whipped the boy across the back as part of the ritual. "On your strength and discomfort you must focus," the Shaman intoned. "Guidance from the Great Spirit, that is what you must ask for." Seemi cringed away from the Alder bough and screeched, "You're hurting me." However, even as he tried to lean away from the striking switch, Spirit Singer swung with greater intensity and frequency, showing his irritation with the boy.

Disgusted at his own violent emotions, Spirit Singer finally threw the branch to the ground and said, "Our lodge is unclean, and that is what the spirits tell me. Purification is what is required. To purify our lodge, this is what they ask of you. Start by emptying all the waste pots. Wash them all well. That is what you must do."

Morning Star in front of the fish drying rack

The Legend of Elos Mountain

Seemi ran to the campfire and stood shivering next to Morning Star, who was positioning a large rack of salmon into the smoke from the fire. Between chattering teeth, Seemi said, "Hello Morning Star."

Morning Star responded, "Hello Seemi," as she continued with her work.

Intent on impressing the girl, Seemi bragged, "I have learned strength and endurance today."

"Oh really?" she asked. "Strength and endurance, that's nice," she said, rolling her eyes as she looked away.

"I am being taught by my uncle, Spirit Singer, about the wisdom in the Circle of Feathers. You know, so that someday I will wear the Circle of Feathers."

Nearby, No Face beached his canoe and unloaded his catch of abalone.

Spirit Singer approached and saw that Seemi was warming himself by the fire and yelled at him. "Is that what the spirits told you to do?"

"I was just checking to see if Morning Star needed help with the fish," he answered.

Spirit Singer said sternly, "Boy, lodge purification. That is what you were told to do."

"I'll take care of that right away," he said turning back to Morning Star and smiling. "I have to be going now. My uncle has important work for me in the lodge."

Morning Star fought back a laugh as Seemi turned and yelled at No Face who had just dropped his load of abalone near the campfire for the women to clean. Seemi took an imperious tone and said, "No Face! Come with me slave. We have work to do."

Chapter One

In front of each lodge was an imposing totem pole, featuring stacked animal heads carved from a single tree. In the village common area, between the campfire and first row of lodges, a group of artisans worked on a 16-foot totem, beginning to take shape from a cedar log.

On the way to his lodge, Spirit Singer wanted to see what progress was being made on the totem poles. The shaman's brother-in-law, Slow Raven, stood with his arms folded. He was doing what he did best, watching other people work and telling them how to do it better and faster. The wood workers used stone axes to chop away large sections of the tree. For the fine work on the faces and bodies of the animals, they used wild cherry wood to create mallets and carving tools tipped with Abalone shell.

Spirit Singer spoke to his brother-in-law sternly, "Working as well as overseeing is what is expected of you. If standing and watching is all you can do, I will put someone else in charge of this important work." Grumbling, Slow Raven picked up his stone axe and joined the other workers. Satisfied, Spirit Singer moved on, pausing at the location of a second totem. He noted that it was nearing completion. It contained the carving of a giant grizzly holding a good-sized salmon. Salmon was very important to the tribe. This figure was nearly ready to have paint applied. The shaman nodded with satisfaction. The first steps in producing black paint were underway. The workers lay limbs of maple and wild cherry in a trench.

As Spirit Singer watched, they brought torches from the main campfire and lit the stack of maple and wild cherry. They covered the fire with green ferns, causing the wood to smolder, producing charcoal. Once the charcoal had cooled, the artisans pounded it to a fine powder and added hot fish oil to get a smooth consistency for the dark paint. In a second fire pit, white paint was nearly ready. Burnt clamshells were removed from the fire pit. They pounded the shells to powder and again added fish oil.

Shortly, the shaman paused where women from the Bear Clan made red paint by mixing the juice of salmon berries, boiled down and mixed with fish oil. Members of the same group were preparing yellow paint from the pulverized roots of wild grape, boiled down and now ready for mixing.

Spirit Singer, having completed his inspection, followed the two boys to the lodge. As Spirit Singer entered, Seemi was ordering No Face to get to work.

"I need this place cleaned up. Wash the cooking pots and then empty all the waste pots."

No Face picked up a cooking pot and started for the door, when Spirit Singer grabbed his arm.

"Stop," cried the Shaman. Then he turned to his nephew, saying, "You were told to do the cleaning. It was not your slave. Now do as you were told, or you will be severely punished."

Chapter One

Seemi grumbled and half-heartedly began arranging some clay pots. As he lifted a very large pot filled with waste, he heard a rattling noise. Seemi looked down to see a timber rattler coiled to strike. Frightened, Seemi screamed and threw the waste pot down, flinging human waste across the room. Some of it splashed up onto Spirit Singer's face.

The Shaman jumped to his feet enraged. Spirit Singer yelled at Seemi, "You are worthless!!"

Seemi cried "Snake, Snake." And ran out of the lodge. He left Spirit Singer and No Face to look for the animal.

The snake slithered across the room and headed out the door after Seemi. No Face ran to the door after it. Spirit Singer stopped to wipe the excrement from his face.

Outside, Seemi yelled a warning to the village, "Rattlesnake, Rattlesnake." Seemi turned and saw the snake emerge from the lodge entrance. It slithered through the dust, heading straight for where Seemi was standing. Seemi ran toward the campfire, as No Face emerged from the lodge. Seeing Seemi in such a state of fright, the villagers began to panic, running in crisscross patterns through the common area. The snake dodged the running humans and just barely got away.

Seemi grabbed a burning branch from the fire and waved it around like a torch. Seeing the fiery stick, the snake changed direction. He headed towards the tall grass that lined the edge of the bare common area. Seemi took a few tentative steps in pursuit of the retreating snake, and then threw the burning torch into the grass. This started a small grass fire. A gust of wind quickly fanned the flames and sent them burning out of control and up the side of Elos Mountain.

Morning Star rushed past Seemi with a blanket and tried to beat out the fire. Caught between the fire and the shouting humans, the snake paused for a moment trying to see which way to go. Suddenly, someone picked up the snake. Filled with fear, the snake turned to strike, and saw the face of a young Indian boy. Before the snake could react, No face tossed the serpent over the burning grass into the tree line. The fire built in intensity, and Morning Star backed away to avoid being burned. Spirit Singer emerged from his lodge to see the hot orange tongues spread to nearby trees, igniting twigs and advancing up the side of Elos Mountain.

Chapter Two
The Great Fire

The fire consumed the foothills of Elos Mountain.
Leaping from tree to tree, tongues of flame raced on,
goaded by winds created by the fire itself. In the hills above
the fire, a dark brown, silver backed grizzly bear raised
his head from a rotten log, where he had been digging for
grubs. Catching the first scent of the fire, the coarse hairs
on his neck rose like signals in the wind. Instantly alert to
the danger, the grizzly turned and prepared to flee. Smoke
obscured the path away from the fire. The bear snorted his
bewilderment and turned full circle, trying to determine
which way to go.

At that moment, flames erupted on the path. The
fire had leapt up the mountain, and then changed direction, trapping Bear. He began digging furiously into the
hardpacked earth. Clumps of dirt and rocks flew out from
between his legs. The hole was only a few feet deep as
the roaring inferno approached. The bear hunkered down
into the shallow hole. He tried to shield himself from the
flames. The sound was a deafening cacophony of crackling
and exploding trees.

Suddenly the world around him erupted as an entire
tree exploded in a hellish holocaust of flame and flying

debris. However, even with his head buried in the shallow hole, the air began to burn the grizzly's lungs. He struggled for each breath. Hot cinders burned his back and singed the fur on his legs. Instinctively, he turned and raged at the fire. A large falling tree landed across his head, driving his body down into the makeshift depression. The bear lost consciousness and drifted off into an eerie black sleep.

When Bear awoke from his dreamless nightmare, he slowly tried climbing out of the hole. However, the fallen tree blocked his movement. The fire had blackened his wooly coat. Bear could feel the deep burns on his back and shoulders. His burned eyelids were shut. He licked his paws and tried to wipe his eyes. Bear grunted in pain and growled faintly. Slowly sliding his haunches from side to side, he began moving dirt away from him to either side of the pit. Bear was finally able to free his head from the embrace of the burned tree. Painfully he pulled himself from the hole that had partially sheltered him. He sat upright, leaning on the edge of the hole to rest.

After a few moments he stood, sniffing the air. With his eyes sightless, he felt his way through the burned forest. He staggered and fell a few times. Bear stopped and sniffed the air. Following his nose, Bear came across the scorched carcass of a deer. He smelled the burned flesh and tore away a large chunk with his powerful jaws. As he chewed, Bear heard a whisper of sound coming from the ground near the carcass. He stopped chewing and listened. He heard the sound again. Growling a warning, Bear stood on his powerful hind legs in a threatening gesture. He listened again, and this time he heard a faint rattle.

Dropping down to all fours, Bear listened intently.

A few inches from his nose, a battered and burned rattlesnake lay, ready to strike. The snake said, "First I'm almost trampled to death and now I'm burned so bad I can hardly crawl. If you're looking for a fight, just put me out of my misery."

Chapter Two

Bear moved his head from side to side, trying to determine just where the voice was coming from.

"I'm right here in front of your nose," Snake whispered. "Are you blind or something? If you do not kill me, I will strike you. In your condition, that bite could be fatal. So, if you want to live, you must kill me."

Bear sniffed the snake, recognized him and said, "Bear doesn't like snakes. We are enemies. Snake tried to bite Bear last year."

"That's because you almost stepped on me, and you've got those huge feet."

Bear was silent for a moment, and then replied, "Bear will not attack Snake now. Bear must find water. Eyes burn. Can't see."

Snake responded, "You can't just leave me here. You have to kill me. My burns are too bad. I can't crawl fast enough to catch prey. I'll die a slow death from starvation."

Bear swung his head from side to side, pondering the situation. Then he asked, "Can Snake see?"

"Yes," Snake replied, "but that doesn't do me any good since I can hardly move."

After another pause, Bear said, "Bear can walk, but can't see. Snake can see but can't crawl." There was only silence from Snake. Then Bear continued speaking. "Bear and Snake could work together. We do not have to be enemies. Bear will find food for Snake. Snake will tell Bear which way to go. Snake will get better. Bear will get better too."

Snake did not answer. After a few moments, Bear shrugged and prepared to move on.

Suddenly Snake responded, "Wait! First, you are going the wrong way.

There is water in the other direction, and perhaps some food. I will get better when I shed my skin and may not be as bad off as I am now. We have an agreement. Snake slowly inched his way towards Bear.

"Bend down that big head of yours."

Bear followed the instructions and Snake slowly worked his way, painstakingly around Bear's neck. The forked tongue gently tickled Bear's ear, and then he spoke. In order to find water, you must follow my direction." Snake explained.

Bear grunted and nodded his head.

When I hiss, you must turn this way," said the snake, touching bear's right shoulder.

Again, Bear grunted and nodded his head in agreement.

Chapter Two

I'll rattle my tail when you need to turn that way," he said, touching Bear's left shoulder with his tail, which gave off a rattling sound that sent a shiver down Bear's back.

Bear can do that," was the response.

"Good," said the snake. "By the way, you can call me Snakey."

"Just call me Bear," was the reply.

"Okay, then go that way," Snakey indicated with a shake of his tail that Bear should go to his left to head toward the water.

Bear followed Snakey's directions, ambling and stumbling down the ash covered hill of burned trees and underbrush. Stepping on a live ember, Bear growled with pain and lifted himself onto his back legs. Snakey hung on tightly, then complained, "be careful you great oaf! You'll drop me if you can't stay on your clumsy feet."

Stung by his companion's words, Bear responded angrily, "Bear will not drop Snake, unless Snakey keeps saying bad things. Then Bear will find the buzzards and leave Snakey with them."

Snakey replied contritely, "Look, I'm sorry. I never worked with a bear before. I may be somewhat short tempered. I will admit it. I would never have thought you were the big sensitive type. I mean no way."

Chapter Three
The Kiltook Village Faces the
Devastation

Spirit Singer, Seemi and No Face stood by the edge of the village and surveyed the fire damage. Spirit Singer turned to Seemi and said, "A meeting of the council has been called for tonight by the Chief, to discuss the fire. You will be there Seemi." The Shaman's words shocked Seemi. He turned to look at No Face with a look of dread. Spirit Singer continued, "A lesson, we'll let this be. Bad things happen. Bad things we cannot prevent. Such a fire could destroy the entire village. A sign, however, is what this is. The Spirits are troubled," Spirit Singer reached into a sealskin bag and removed a rattle, shaped like a bird. He danced and shook the rattle in the air around Seemi's body, as he intoned, "Great spirits of the trees, the animals, the flowers and the small creatures. Your return is what we ask. Re-birth is what we need."

Spirit Singer finished his brief prayer, reached into his pouch, and removed a handful of seeds. He held the handful of seeds in the air and prayed, "With these seeds I sow, bless our people and rejuvenate the forest and bring back life."

Spirit Singer scattered the seeds into the wind. A few of them fell at the feet of Seemi and No Face. Spirit Singer then reached down and grabbed a mixture of earth and seeds. He then motioned Seemi to follow his example. "Do as I do. You must learn."

Seemi reached down and grabbed some earth and seeds. As Seemi stepped forward closer to his uncle, No Face leaned down and grabbed a small handful of the mixture. Spirit Singer continued, "This has the potential for

Chapter Three

life. Examine what is in the palm of your hand. Concentrate all your will on the seeds and bring forth life." Seemi stared at the dirt and seeds in his hand, but nothing happened. He concentrated his glare by moving his head closer to his open palm.

No Face looked at the mixture in his own hand. He closed his eyes and then closed his fist around the dirt. Seemi looked at the shaman and said, "Nothing is happening, uncle. How long does it take?"

"Patience, that is what you must have," Spirit Singer replied.

No Face opened his eyes and looked into his hand. He smiled as a tiny sprout sprang forth.

Spirit Singer saw the sprout of green in No Face's hand and exclaimed, "Oh." The shaman was suddenly aware that the slave had more sensitivity and spiritual potential than his lazy minded nephew. Seemi looked up to see his uncle staring at No Face.

No Face did not want to upstage his master, as it would bring retribution. But he was suddenly aware that he was capable of gaining the skills that Seemi seemed totally unaware of. No Face quickly emptied the dirt onto the ground.

Meanwhile, back in the burned forest, Bear could smell the water and tried to walk faster. Snakey kept giving directions. He rattled his tail and Bear turned left. "Turn farther," said Snakey, rattling his tail harder. "Now go the other way," he said with a hiss. "Now you must jump!"

"How far," Bear asked, but it was too late. He fell over a log and rolled down the slope. Snakey clung tightly to his neck. When Bear stopped rolling, he could feel cool mud beneath his scorched feet. He followed his nose to the water's edge and waded out into the rushing current. Snakey tried to keep his head above water, as Bear engulfed himself in the cool liquid, bathing his wounds. Bear then lowered his head down into the water.

"Oh no, here we go," thought Snakey. Under the water, Bear was finally able to open his burned eyelids. When he raised his head above the surface, his eyes were blistered white.

Snake struggled for air and sputtered, "Are you trying to drown me or something? Give me a little warning next time."

"Bear's eyes are open, but Bear cannot see," the Grizzly growled.

Snakey looked at Bear's milky white eyeballs. Shocked by what he saw, he said, "Oh my."

Bear asked worriedly, "What is wrong with Bear's eyes?"

"Oh nothing," Snakey replied. "I think your eyes will heal nicely."

"Why does Snakey say, 'Oh my'?" Bear asked.

Snakey gave an involuntary shake of his head and said, "Well, you look a little scary right now. But then again, you were always scary." Bear seemed satisfied with that answer. "Let's get something straight," said Snakey. "when I hiss once," he said, tapping Bear's right shoulder, "go this way a little. When I hiss loud twice, go farther in that direction. If I want you to go the other way a little," he said, hitting Bear's left shoulder with a rattle of his tail, "I'll just tap you with my rattle once. If I want to go farther, I'll tap you twice with my rattle," he said, once again hitting Bear's left shoulder with his tail.

"Bear can do that." was the reply. Then he changed the subject, saying, "Bear does not know if it is night or day."

Snakey looked around at the smoky haze that surrounded them and answered, "It's twilight I think. Though it's hard to tell, because the fire has filled the air with smoke and the forest is still burning higher up on the mountain."

Bear shook his head from side to side in agitation. "Bear needs to find food for Snake and Bear. But, Bear does not know where to go."

Snakey showed irritation in his voice, saying, "What's with this 'Bear will do this and Bear will do that?' You act as if you are talking about someone else. Say I need to find food. I do not know where to go. Can you say I?" The grizzly sounded defensive, saying, "Of course Bear can say I."

"There you go again Bear," Snakey said in exasperation.

"Bear doesn't understand," he said, shaking his mighty head from side to side.

"See! You're doing it right now," Snakey replied.

"Bear is doing what?"

"Okay, forget it." Snakey replied. "The wind has chased the fire to the south surely if we travel north, we can find where the forest was spared."

Bear thought about it for a moment, and then snorted, "Bear will go north." He took a couple of steps down the slope.

"Ah, north is the other way," Snakey retorted. "Where would you be without me?"

"Where would Snakey be without Bear," was the reply. He turned his giant frame around and began walking. "That way a bit more," said Snakey with one tap of his rattle on Bear's left shoulder. "That's good," Snakey responded. "That's very good."

Working together, they avoided another tree that blocked their way. Snakey surveyed Bear's wounds. "By the way," said Snakey. "You're looking kind of moth eaten, Bear. The fire burned a lot of the fur off your shoulders and legs."

Bear snorted his unhappiness and responded, "The fire burned Bear. It hurts when Bear walks."

Snakey replied sarcastically, "The lady bears will surely scorn your attention in the future, should you ever be so lucky as to have one cross your path."

"Bear does not care now. Bear will heal, then find lady bear. Snakey will never find lady snake. Snakey is too mean."

"Okay, okay. I guess I deserved that," Snakey replied. He suddenly noticed a fallen tree blocking their path and said, "This way," said Snakey with a hiss. "Turn a little more." Bear complied. Then Snakey said loudly, "Get ready to jump."

"How far?" asked Bear.

"Not too far," Snakey responded. Bear jumped and easily avoided the smoldering tree.

Chapter Four
TheFire Starter Named

No Face is Blamed

The burned area to the south of the village was visible in the twilight. The village itself was safe, but the scorched landscape around it extended all the way up the slopes of Elos Mountain. Various villagers gathered at the entrance to the Chief's Lodge, which was the largest Lodge, standing in the center of the village. Inside the roomy structure, a large lodge-pole extended across the inside of the roof. It was held in place by large wooden supports at either end of the

100-foot long building. Strands of dried fish hung from the rafters. The elders, representing the entire village, gathered in a great circle.

Chief Sagawan sat on the platform.

A great-carved wooden statue of a grizzly guarded a raised platform at one end of the room. Chief Sagawan sat cross-legged on the platform. He wore a multi-colored coat, adorned with shells and shark's teeth. His long dark hair was slick with whale oil and covered with bird plumage. Chief Sagwan's family sat to his right on the platform. From this group, Morning Star looked out at the gathering. She saw Seemi standing in the middle of the circle of elders. Spirit Singer handed the talking stick to Chief Sagawan, and then took his place on the platform.

The clan became quiet as the Chief began to speak, "A great fire has eaten the slopes of Elos Mountain. A fire started here in the village. This fire had a powerful spirit, because Spirit Singer, who wears the circle of Feathers, could do nothing to prevent it." Spirit Singer looked down with humility. The Chief continued, "Seemi, the nephew of Spirit

Singer, should know how this fire did come to live." Spirit singer took the talking stick and presented it to Seemi, who fidgeted and shuffled his feet. Seemi took the talking stick and began to ramble incoherently.

"I was ah… Spirit Singer, the Circle of Feathers, the endurance ritual, and then we got abalone for the village, and salmon, we checked on that. I was cleaning, cleaning. Then a snake. It came at me. It almost got me. I'm lucky to be alive. However, my slave No Face, chased the snake with a torch and started the fire." Morning Star glared at Seemi. She looked around for No Face, but the slave was not in the room to make a defense.

Chief Sagawan responded, "It should be that these things you say are the truth Seemi."

The boy answered, "Ah, yes. Yes, it's the truth." "Then we should see your slave No Face," said the Chief. Seemi hurried out of the lodge. Morning Star leaned to whisper to the chief, "Father." Sagawan turned and glared at his daughter, raising his hand for her to be quiet. Morning Star spoke anyway, "He didn't do it Father. He did not do it."

Morning Star knew
Seemi had lied.

Chief Sagawan said sternly, "We must respect the word of Seemi, the nephew of Spirit Singer, our great Circle of Feathers."

Seemi entered the lodge, pushing No Face before him into the center of the circle.

Chief Sagawan spoke, You are the slave, No Face?"

No Face responded, "Yes."

Sagawan continued. "you have caused a great disaster to befall this village. You have angered the spirit of Elos Mountain. You should be punished for what you have done." The Chief looked at Seemi, who was standing on the edge of the circle, and asked, "Do you have anything to say on behalf of your slave before we decide his punishment?"

Seemi stepped forward into the circle. He caught a glimpse of Morning Star as she concentrated her glare, then he spoke, "I think the slave thought he was helping me. He was trying to kill the snake, but I was not afraid of the snake. My slave thought I needed help. I will punish him for the harm he has caused."

The Chief drew the Elders to one side and they discussed the situation. After a few minutes, Chief Sagawan stood and said, "We have talked on this. And it will be as Seemi says."

Seemi left the Chief's lodge, pushing No Face ahead of him. When they arrived back at Spirit Singer's lodge, Seemi tied No Face to a post outside the lodge. Taking a stick from his belt, Seemi began beating No Face across his back and shoulders. After a dozen lashes. Seemi put the stick back in his belt and entered the lodge, closing the door behind him.

No Face remained tied to the post. Slowly, he inched his way into a sitting position to wait through the night.

Spirit Singer emerged from the lodge and walked quietly to where No Face was slumped against the whipping post. He looked down at the bruised and bleeding slave boy. No Face peered up at the Shaman solemnly, but remained silent. Spirit Singer patted the boy's head.

Chapter Five
Nighttime back in the Forest

A nice fat mouse would do.

Bear and Snakey finally reached the living part of the forest. The scent of berries instantly attracted Bear to some nearby bushes.

Snakey said, "Hey, blackerries are great and all, but I don't eat blackberries. You got that?"

Bear continued chomping, but spoke with his mouth full, "What do you want?" he asked.

"A nice fat mouse would do, so catch one for me," said Snakey. Bear finished a few more bites and then began to sniff for a mouse.

"Bear doesn't smell a mouse," he said, turning back towards the blackberries.

"Get down lower. They live in holes, stupid," said Snakey in exasperation.

"Snakey should not call Bear stupid," he growled.

"Okay, Okay," Snakey, replied.

"Get down lower, please?" Bear leaned down and sniffed the earth. After a few snorts, he detected something odd. "What is it? You got something?" Snakey asked.

Bear replied, "Tamba has been here."

"Who is Tamba?" Snakey wanted to know.

"Tamba is Bear's enemy. Tamba is bad. Tamba attacked Bear."

Tamba, Bear's Enemy.

"Well then, we should find shelter for the night." Said Snakey.

"Snakey is not hungry?" asked Bear.

"I can wait until tomorrow," was the reply. "Snakes only eat every once in a while."

"Bear did not know that."

"We can see in the dark too," said Snakey.

"Snakey is a good hunter," Bear responded.

Bear began walking. Snakey hardly had to navigate at all. Bear had learned to sense and smell his way around most of the larger obstacles.

"You're getting pretty good at this," Snakey remarked. "You've got a good nose."

"But Snakey has good eyes," Bear replied.

"A bit more that way," Snakey interjected with a tap of his rattles.

Bear veered to the left, following the path along the ledge of a dangerous precipice. Snakey, who had been snuggled deeply into Bear's rich neck fur, poked his head out to look down at the rocky chasm below. "Bear is doing okay?" Bear asked.

"A-O-K," was the response. The trail suddenly veered away from the ledge and led into the forest. Snakey silently sighed in relief. After a few more steps, Bear stopped suddenly and sniffed. "What is it? Snakey asked. "Do you smell a nice mouse?"

"No, Bear smells a cave," was the reply.

"Maybe there will be mice in there. Where is it?"

Bear continued walking ahead slowly, sniffing the ground. "Cave smells close," said Bear. Following his nose, as the scent grew stronger. Bear suddenly tumbled headfirst into a hole.

Snakey, hissed furiously and rattled his tail in fright. He lost his hold on Bear's neck and fell head over tail into the pit below.

Bear roared in fear.

Bear roared in fear and rage, chomping his jaws, as if he faced an imaginary enemy. His front feet were dangling in the air, while his back feet were maintaining a tenuous grip on the edge of the hole. "Snakey! Where are you?" Listening for a reply, Bear heard a faint hiss from the depths below. Bear called out, "Snakey, are you there?" Bear listened intently.

"Yeah, it's me," was the weak response.

"Where are you?" Bear asked.

"I'm about 10 feet below you. I cannot crawl to you. Are you stuck?" Snakey asked.

Bear used his back legs for advantage and answered, "Bear can get out." Bear tried not to despair over their mutual predicament. He struggled with all his great strength, to back out of the hole. The earth around him shifted as he dug in with his huge rear feet, pulling with all his might. Then with one mighty tug, he was out.

Snakey felt a sense of panic and cried out, "Bear" Don't leave me here. I am sorry I called you names and said you were stupid. I know I was rude sometimes. I want to apologize for that." Suddenly a mouse appeared on a rock, about a foot in front of Snakey's head. He quickly struck, like a whip, and the mouse was gone. As Snakey was slowly swallowing his meal, clods of dirt began raining down into the cave. Snakey called out, "Hey! What's going on?"

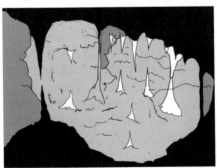
The entrance to a giant Cavern.

Bear used his mighty front paws to dig out and enlarge the cave entrance. As he dug, great clumps of earth fell down into the opening. At one point, Bear smelled a nice tuber root with an appetizing aroma. He stopped digging for a moment, to eat. From below, he could hear Snakey calling,

"Bear? What are you doing?"

The answer came back, "Bear will dig. Then Bear will come and get Snakey."

"Then why aren't you digging?" Snakey asked.

"A big rock is blocking the hole. Bear will move the rock." Bear sniffed the large boulder that guarded the cave entrance. Carefully he dug his way around the huge rock. Bear called, "Look out, Snakey." Lowering his rear legs into the hole, Bear inched past the rock until he was directly below it. Then pressing his body upwards with a mighty heave of his shoulders and forelegs, he pushed the rock up and out of the cave entrance. Now, with plenty of space, Bear dropped to the bottom of the cave. There was room for him to turn a complete circle. He asked, "Snakey, are you okay?"

Snakey wiggled his head out from under a pile of earth, spitting dirt. "Yuk – yes, I'm okay." Bear turned toward the direction of Snakey's voice and took a step.

"That's far enough," Snakey hissed. "Move a little closer to me and put your head down so I can climb back on."

Bear followed Snakey's instructions.

Snakey, painstakingly, coiled himself around Bear's neck, then asked, "Can you climb back out of here?"

"Bear can climb out," was the answer. Bear began to claw up the sides of the pit. As he lifted his body up off the floor of the cave, a sudden wind current blew his fur.

"That's odd," said Snakey. "You feel that breeze? It's coming from inside the cave."

Bear stopped climbing and dropped back to the cave floor. He sniffed the moving air and followed it to a sidewall, where a small hole gushed with the air current. Bear breathed the air deeply and then suddenly began digging.

Snakey asked, "What are you doing?" Bear did not answer. As he dug, the hole opened up and the perimeter of the opening crumbled away, revealing the entrance to a giant cavern.

Inside, Snakey could see giant stalactites hanging from the ceiling of the cave. Snakey whispered, "It's a huge cave with those hangy things up above that drip water."

Bear stepped into the cavern and walked without any direction from Snakey. He maneuvered around rock formations with his nose in the air, leading the way.

Snakey asked, "Where are we going? This place is Creepy."

Snakey said, "You're not going to believe this."

Bear stopped and deeply smelled the cavern floor. "Bear smells bones; fresh bones; old bones." Bear turned completely around, sniffing the air, and then began walking deeper into the cavern.

Chapter Five

Snakey looked around the odd shaped cave formations. He occasionally glance ahead to make sure they were not going to hit anything. Seeing a large stalagmite rising from the floor ahead, Snakey decided to issue a warning. Snakey said, "Ah, there's a..." Before he could finish his sentence, bear sniffed the air ahead and made a slight adjustment to their course. They narrowly walked between two stalagmites dripping with calciferous water. Snakey heard the sound of breaking bones. He looked down to see that Bear was walking through a circle of bones. He watched as a large femur shattered under the tremendous weight of Bear's body. Bear came to a halt in the center of the circle.

Snakey looked up to see something incredible. Snakey said, "You're not going to believe this."

Bear sniffed the air once again and nodded his head, then replied. "It's the bones of a very old bear." Directly in front of Bear and Snakey, was a complete skeleton of a huge prehistoric bear, twice Bear's size. Bear lay down on the cave floor next to the pile of bones. He gave a quiet sigh and fell instantly asleep.

Snakey looked around quizzically and asked, "We spending the night here? This place is kinda spooky." Snakey extended his head out to see Bear's closed eyes and heard his heavy breathing. "I guess so," the snake muttered. "Oh well." Snakey relaxed his body and dropped to the cool floor of the cave. He curled up with his nose next to his nine rattles and tried to keep awake, but he began to fall asleep without wanting to. Smelling the air, he tried once more to fight sleep. He lost the battle and fell into a deep trance like sleep.

Chapter Six
The Sky over Gondwanaland

Snakey was flying through the heavens, high above Gondwanaland. The earth below was all one giant continent. Looking down, he could see everything happening below. Groups of aborigines were painting a picture on a cliff wall. It was the picture of men walking and hunters with spears among what appeared to be cattle or oxen.

Men walking and hunters with spears.

On an adjacent wall was a picture of a flying snake. Snakey realized he was no longer in pain. He stretched out his long body. Twisting his head to look back, he could see that from his tail to his nose, he stretched halfway around the world. The earth moved and shifted from the shock waves caused by his movements in the air. Below, a small piece of the continent broke away to form Tasmania. Another chunk separated to become New Guinea. The tectonic plates moved and folded over, tearing the great Gondwanaland into seven large pieces. Snakey moved down slowly to earth and carved great valleys with his body, forcing the land on each side of him to form new mountain ranges.

A boy appeared on the top of one of the newly formed mountains. Snakey paused for a moment, as the boy spoke, "Your time here will be remembered for eternity. Where I am is the real world. Where you are is the dream world. You shall be the totem for the Giver of sight."

Snakey then effortlessly stretched his body high into the ionosphere, and disappeared into the heavens.

Back in the cave, it was still night. A misty snake soul coiled itself into a circle. Slowly it materialized back into earthly form on the floor of the cave next to Bear, as he slept inside the circle of bones. Bear shifted into a different position as he slept. Sensing movement in the cavern, Bear opened his eyes and realized he could see. Suddenly a bright light from a hole in the ceiling illuminated the cave. Standing in the light, towering high above the sleepy Bear was the prehistoric Cave Bear. He bent his enormous head down and nuzzled Bear. Bear rolled over on his back submissively, as if he were a playful cub.

The Cave Bear spoke, "You have chosen your companion well. Together, the two of you will bring life back to the forest. This will be your life quest!" The Cave Bear stood on his hind legs, stretching his body almost to the ceiling of the great cavern, then continued speaking, "You must visit all the spirits of the forest, the plants, trees, insects, and animals. You will guide them all back to their homes. And when you are finished, I will restore your sight."

Bear rolled back to his feet and stood on his hind legs mimicking his ancient ancestor. Snakey woke up and looked around to find Bear standing up. He seemed to be peering up, though his eyes were closed. It was as if he could see.

Snakey figured he was sleepwalking. Snakey called out, "Hey Bear, hey. Wake up." Bear opened his milky eyes and wagged his head from side to side, trying to figure out where he was. Snakey said, "You were sleep-walking."

"Bear is sorry," the grizzly responded. Bear sat back down and said, "Bear dreamed that he could see."

"Your eyes will heal. Don't worry," Snakey assured him.

Bear nodded his head and said, "Bear will see, when life comes back to the forest." The grizzly lowered his head and Snakey inched his way around Bear's neck. Bear then stood and walked towards the entrance of the cave.

"What's going on?" Snakey asked. "Where are we going? – Hey look out, there's one of those pointy things in the way," he said, giving a little hiss to indicate a slight turn to the right. Bear changed course slightly as Snakey indicated and easily missed the stalagmite.

Chapter Seven
No Face at the Whipping Post

No Face was alone, still tied to the whipping post, in the cold night. A bright full moon illuminated the village. As he lay slumped on the ground, he heard a sound and raised his head. It was Morning Star.

She knelt down next to him and offered him some food and water.

He thirstily gulped the water, spilling it down his chin, where it dripped onto his chest. No Face spoke, "Thank you." Morning Star put her hand over his mouth and shook her head for him to be silent. Then she slowly put a piece of bread into his mouth and he chewed with intense satisfaction. He looked into her eyes and smiled. Morning Star smiled back and then stroked his cheek.

No Face closed his eyes and relished her touch. Standing in the doorway of his lodge, Spirit Singer observed the interchange between No Face and Morning Star. A wry smile crossed his lips. He then cleared his throat softly and made some purposeful noise from his position in the doorway.

Morning Star scurried away, hoping to avoid detection. No Face felt sad. He look up at the beautiful moon. "Oh beautiful moon, hide your face from me, so you will not see my tears."

No Face looked up at the beautiful moon.

Spirit Singer heard No Face's supplication and noticed the light from the moon begin to dim. He looked to see the beginning of a lunar eclipse. Spirit Singer called out in a loud voice, "All who hear my voice, come and witness the spirits giving us a sign."

Spirit Singer: "All who hear my voice."

Several other members of the tribe appeared in their doorways. They looked to the sky and pointed, as the moon slowly disappeared from view. One of the villagers approached Spirit Singer and asked, "Oh great Circle of Feathers, what are we to do? The moon is being swallowed by a giant fish." The villager pointed to a narrow band of clouds that looked very much like a fish swallowing up the last sliver of the moon.Spirit Singer was still looking at No Face in amazement. He realized that this boy had a natural gift of spiritual sensitivity and awareness that rivalled his own. This thought left him with the realization that No Face should have been the one in training to replace him as the Circle of Feathers. He turned to the villagers saying, "A display of great power is before our eyes, but no harm will come to you or to our people."

The next morning, Seemi left the lodge and pulled his black obsidian knife from his belt. He cut the thongs that bound No Face to the Whipping Post. No Face rubbed his arms and stretched out the cold and stiffness in his body. Seemi said, "I must provide meat for the village. Go get my bow and arrows and the other supplies. We are going on a hunt." No Face entered the lodge, leaving Seemi outside to wait. As Seemi waited, Morning Star approached, carrying a bundle of sticks. She stopped and glared at Seemi.

Seemi glared at Morning Star.

"What are you looking at?" Seemi demanded. Morning Star did not speak, but concentrated her scowl. Seemi again demanded, "What is wrong with you?"

"You falsely accused No Face for something you did. You lied before my father and the council," she responded angrily.

Seemi was shocked that she would have the nerve to make such an accusation. "I don't know what you are talking about," he said in a low angry tone.

"You know exactly what I'm talking about. You started that fire. You did it," she hissed. "Then you blamed it on No Face because you weren't man enough to take responsibility for it yourself. You were not man enough! You are nothing but a coward."

Seemi took a step forward and leaned down into Morning Star's face. She did not back down. "Listen to me girl," he warned. "You may be Sagawan's daughter, but I am a man, and you are nothing but a girl. No one will dispute my word against yours. I suggest you keep your opinions to yourself." Seemi turned and walked away, just as No Face appeared with the equipment. "Let's go No Face. I must provide meat for the village."

Morning Star remained steadfast in Seemi's path. As he turned to walk past her, she threw her bundle of sticks to the ground, scattering them in his way.

Seemi ignored the obstacles and walked through the sticks," stepping over those he could. No Face stopped to help Morning Star pick them up. "Leave the sticks," Seemi ordered his slave. "Come with me. We have more important work." No Face obeyed. Then he turned for one last look at Morning Star, before they rounded the corner of Spirit Singer's lodge and disappeared.

Deep in the forest, the two boys stopped at the edge of a clearing. Seemi and No Face crouched behind a bush, watching a deer. Seemi positioned his bow and held out his hand for an arrow. No Face gave him an arrow from the quiver he carried. Seemi strung the arrow and pulled back on the gut string, taking aim at the deer that had stopped to eat some grass. As the animal moved to one side, Seemi released the arrow, which twisted through the air and missed the buck by ten feet. The deer looked around for a moment, but then continued to eat. Seemi demanded another arrow and took aim for a second shot. He pulled back and released the arrow. The shot missed the deer by ten feet in the opposite direction. Once again, the deer looked up, surveyed the clearing and continued eating. Seemi loaded a third arrow and took aim. Then he released it, the arrow hit a tree ten feet in front of them. The sound spooked the deer and he ran into the forest. Seemi jumped to his feet, exclaiming, "I must get him."

Seemi and No Face ran after the deer, which dodged and leapt through the forest ahead of them. As they ran, Seemi released several more arrows that all missed their mark. Suddenly the deer came to an abrupt halt. It sniffed the air, its nostrils pumping as it smelled the scent of a bear. The deer then turned and ran directly at Seemi and No Face, charging them as if it meant to attack. Seemi yelled, "It's coming right at me, give me an arrow."

No Face handed him an arrow and said, "That's the last one."

"You stupid slave," Seemi screamed. "Why didn't you bring more arrows?"

"I brought all your arrows," No Face answered.

As the deer raced towards them, Seemi took aim. At the last second, he released the arrow. It hit the deer in the chest and pierced its heart. The animal tumbled to the ground with the horns coming to rest a few feet from where the two boys stood.

Seemi gave a victorious whoop, "Eeeahhh!! I killed the deer! I am a great hunter!" He then stepped over to the dead deer to check his trophy and said, "No Face, go find all my arrows. I don't want to lose a single one."

No Face turned and hurried back and began searching the undergrowth for the lost arrows.

Chapter Eight
Bear's Mortal Enemy Tamba appears

Tamba headed towards the scent of
the Deer,

A short distance away, a seven-foot black bear, Tamba, sniffed the air. Smelling a deer, he headed in the direction of the scent.

Back in the cave, Bear was digging and clawing with all his might to get up the walls of the hole that led out of the cave. Each time he got part way up, he began sliding back down.

Snakey remarked. "I thought you said you could climb out of here?"

"Bear can do it," the grizzly replied. "Be patient." Bear attempted again, losing his footing, he slid back to the bottom of the pit. Bear stopped to rest and as he was breathing hard, he caught a scent that grabbed his attention and he began sniffing inquisitively.

"What is it?" Snakey asked.

"It's Bear's enemy, Tamba, and he's near."

Chapter Eight

"Maybe we should just stay here until he's gone, suggested Snakey. "You're in no condition for a fight."

Bear stood up, prepared for another attempt, and said, "Bear never hides from a fight." Bear strained and clawed with all his strength. He slowly inched his way upwards, and then he braced all four legs against the walls of the pit and lifted himself up. Digging in with his back legs, he managed to push his head and shoulders over the top and into the fresh air. He wiggled out of the hole and then shook off the soil that clung to his fur.

Snakey hung on for dear life as Bear shivered and shuddered all over, then remarked. "Do you have to do that?"

Bear sniffed the air and determined the direction that Tamba's scent was coming from. Bear said, "Tamba has just killed a deer."

"Are you sure you wouldn't like to deal with it tomorrow?" asked Snakey.

"Something tells Bear, we need to deal with this now." Was the reply.

Meanwhile, back on the trail, Seemi pulled his knife from his belt and stabbed the deer's carcass. He took some of the blood from the wound and smeared it on his face and chest. As he turned to look for No Face, he mumbled, "Stupid slave. Where are you?" Seemi heard a grunt and turned, expecting to see No Face. He was stunned at the sight of Tamba's seven-foot figure looming over him, only a few feet away. Before Seemi could react, Tamba roared loudly and attacked. He swatted Seemi out of the way, sending the boy flying a good ten feet into the bushes. Tamba then attacked the deer tearing flesh from the carcass.

No Face was some distance away when he heard the roar. He turned and began running back to his master. He flew through the forest, jumping and hurdling obstacles. Seemi looked out from the brush where he was cowering and saw Tamba devouring the deer. Seemi hunkered down, trying to keep out of sight. No Face arrived to find Tamba standing over the deer. He looked around and spotted Seemi rolled into a ball behind a bush. He went to Seemi's side as Tamba took notice of the two boys. Tamba stopped eating and stepped over the deer, heading directly for Seemi and No Face. No Face tried to get Seemi to move, but Seemi froze in fear.

Desperate to do something, No Face grabbed Seemi's knife, holding it, prepared to defend his master. Tamba's great body slashed through the bushes directly towards the boys. Suddenly a loud commotion behind Tamba distracted him. Turning to find the source of the clamor, Tamba was astonished to see Bear towering above him. At the sight of his hated enemy, Tamba gave a high pierc-

Chapter Eight

ing scream of rage. He lowered his head and attacked. When Tamba struck, Bear and Snakey rolled with the power of the enraged animal's onslaught. Snakey hissed and rattled his tail furiously in warning as Tamba made a second charge. The two bears locked together in furious combat.

No Face was in shock. The second animal was even larger than the first. His attention focused on the ten-foot grizzly and his two milky mooneyes that appeared sightless. As he wateched the fight, he saw the serpent wrapped around the blind bear's neck. It struck out at Tamba, trying to help his companion.

Snakey struck and missed due to Tamba's dense fur and rapid movements.

Tamba tore at Bear's shoulder, making a deep wound. He was, however, distracted for a moment, by the snake's appearance and aggressive actions. Tamba began to dodge the snake's strikes, allowing Bear to make contact. In the process, Bear wounded Tamba's chest.

Almost instantaneously, Snakey made contact with Tamba's nose, sinking his fangs deeply into the soft tissue and injecting his venom.

Tamba screamed in pain and pulled back, dragging the still attached snake away from Bear's neck. He clawed at his own face, causing deep wounds as he finally managed to remove Snakey, who fell to the ground.

Tamba once again charged into Bear and they locked together, wrestling for a final death hold. It appeared that Tamba was getting the best of the fight, now that Snakey was injured.

Seeing this, No Face was compelled to do something. He grasped the knife tightly, rushed up behind the attacking Tamba, and with all his might, sunk the knife to the hilt in Tamba's lower back. Then pulled it out and prepared for a second thrust.

No Face pulled out the knife and prepared for a second thrust.

Tamba screamed in agony, stopped fighting and ran away into the forest as fast as his wounds would allow. Bear stood on his hind legs, sniffing the air, and then, catching the scent of the human, he chomped his jaws, preparing for yet another attack.

"Bear, wait," Snakey called out. Bear turned toward the sound of his fallen comrade. "The human helped us fight off Tamba," said Snakey.

Where are you?" asked Bear.

"Follow my voice," Snakey replied. Bear began hunting for Snakey, who lay crumpled on the ground near No Face. Snakey said, "bend your head down so I can climb back on." Bear bent down.

No Face stared, dumbfounded by what he saw. The snake was trying to move back around bear's neck. However, his wounds were too severe.

Chapter Eight

No Face leaned over and carefully positioned Snakey around Bear's neck.

No Face puts Snakey back around Bear's neck.

Bear then rose and sniffed the human who stood before him. He moved a little closer, so that No Face stood just a few inches away.

"Kill me if you will great bear from the spirit world. For it must be my destiny."

From his position, hiding in the bushes, Seemi stared in disbelief as Bear stood to his full height, like a mighty vision of power.

As No Face looked up at the grizzly, Bear lowered himself down on all fours. One of his mooneyes peered vacantly at the boy. Suddenly, Bear stretch out his nose and nuzzled No Face gently.

Chapter Nine
Seemi Limps Away

Realizing this was his chance to escape, Seemi climbed to his feet and limped away as fast as he could. He stopped when he reached the creek that flowed down into the village. As he rested, trying to regain his breath, he heard something coming down the trail. Too tired and in too much pain to run, he hid behind a rock and waited. Peering from his hiding place, Seemi was surprised to see No Face come around the corner carrying the deer on his back. Seemi jumped out onto the path to stop the slave. "That's my deer," cried Seemi.

No Face ignored his master. He turned sullenly and continued down the path to the village. Upset by his slave's lack of response, Seemi ran up behind him and tripped No Face, causing him to fall, dropping the deer. No Face left the deer on the ground and regained his feet.

"Am I not your master?" Seemi screamed at him. "I know how you would love to make yourself out to be some kind of hero. You would love to disgrace me in the eyes of my uncle and the entire village. I know you for what you really are. I watched you and that moon-eyed monster. You are in league with evil spirits." Seemi held out his hand and pointed to the knife tucked into No Face's belt. "Give me my knife." Seemi demanded.

No Face slowly took the knife and paused for a moment. He looked down at the blade and then up at Seemi. He then handed the knife to his master.

Seemi tucked the knife away, and then suddenly charged No Face and pushed him off the path into a patch of devil's club. The vicious spikes tore at No Face's body as he fell into the thorny mass. Despite his wounds, Seemi managed to get the deer onto his shoulder and continued down the trail, entering the village.

He stood in the middle of the common area with the deer at his feet. The villagers gathered around and congratulated him.

Spirit Singer and Morning Star watched. They noticed that Seemi was injured. His arm was bleeding and there was blood on his face and chest. "You are hurt," Spirit Singer said. "Tell us, what happened?" "I shot the deer, and then I was attacked by a bear. It hit me and knocked me back and then it went after the deer."

"Where is No Face?" asked Morning Star.

"He is hiding somewhere," replied Seemi. "He was so afraid. But I wasn't about to let that Bear have my deer, so I crept up behind him and stabbed him to death with my knife."

Spirit Singer wrinkled his forehead, not really believing Seemi's story.

Morning Star shook her head 'no' in disbelief.

No Face stumbled into the village, bruised and bleeding. He was exhausted and took a seat outside Spirit Singer's lodge.

Morning Star saw him and smiled, but resisted the urge to go comfort him.

Seemi continued, "I got that deer with my first arrow, right through the heart."

No Face looked up and rolled his eyes as Seemi continued. "And I would say the bear was seven feet tall. He had massive claws and sharp teeth."

Spirit Singer nodded his head knowingly and replied, "Back to where the bear died, that is where we must go. Its hide and meat we must take." Seemi looked at the ground, shuffled his feet and said, "I'm exhausted and I've been injured, perhaps after I've recovered."

Spirit Singer replied with vehemence, "Before the bear's spirit becomes angry. We must take a party there now."

Seemi grudgingly agreed, "Well, um okay, I guess we could go now."

Spirit Singer started preparing for the trip.

No Face slowly climbed to his feet to join the group. Seemi looked at him and said, "You stay here No Face. We don't need you."

A group of warriors, led by Seemi and Spirit Singer searched the trail for the dead bear.

"I think it was around here somewhere. Or, maybe just up the way a bit." The group continued their search. After rounding a corner, they came to a place where the earth was torn, branches were broken and blood was still wet on the ground. Spirit Singer bent down and examined the pool of blood. "The bear was wounded perhaps but dead he is not" stated Spirit Singer. Seemi pulled out his knife and showing it to the others in the party said, "I used this knife. I thought I killed it. It lay motionless after I stabbed it." Seemi pointed to some dried blood still on the knife. "Look, there is the monster's blood. When we find it I will finish the job." In the distance, hunkered down under some brush, was Tamba. He was recovering, panting rapidly and licking his wounds. He looked up and saw Seemi and the group of warriors in the distance. Seemi was holding the knife in the air. Tamba growled quietly, not wanting to take on so many humans at once.

Chapter Nine

Arriving back in the village, Spirit Singer and Seemi walked to the front of the lodge, where they were greeted by a waiting No Face. "The bear is alive," said Spirit Singer. "But I think you already knew that."

No Face remained silent as Seemi glared at him, to make sure he did not respond.

Spirit Singer continued, "A lesson is what was given to you two boys. Communicating with the animals, that is what you must learn. When you are lost, or hungry, or need to keep warm, animals can be powerful allies. Tell me Seemi," Spirit Singer continued, "Seeing a bear, what does that mean?"

"It teaches us how to dream, to build dreams," Seemi answered.

Spirit Singer shook his head, "No, the wisdom to go within is what the bear teaches." Spirit Singer looked up at the sky as a raven appeared. It flew high over the village. He stuck out his hand and made an odd calling sound. The bird suddenly went into a dive, coming to perch on spirit Singer's outstretched arm.

Seemi was amazed that the bird stayed on Spirit Singer's arm and said, "How did you do that uncle? Can I do it too?"

"No, "Spirit Singer replied. "Your true self. That is what you must discover first. There are two worlds. Is it this world, or the spirit world? Which is the real one? This world is only a dream. In the spirit world, that is where your true self lives. Moreover, an animal, that is what your reality will be. So your animal, that is what you must find."

No Face soaked in these words, as Seemi remained focused on the novelty of the bird.

"Can you make the bird do tricks?" Seemi asked.

"No, tricks are for children," Spirit Singer replied. "Serious is what this is. If you can dream the dream of your own animal, then it becomes easier to dream the dreams of other animals, and even humans."

"Like knowing what other people are thinking? I would like that," Seemi responded.

Spirit Singer slowly took a seat on a small wood stool. He then raised his hand up close to the bird's feet and it stepped off his arm and into his hand. He then lowered the bird and deposited it on the ground. The raven twisted its head from side to side, but stayed where Spirit Singer had placed it. "Concentrate on the bird," his uncle directed. "Ask the raven to teach you about the magic. Ask the raven to show you the sacred teachings that it guards. Ask it to show you the void, so you will no longer be afraid."

Seemi leaned forward and drilled his stare into the raven's eyes. The raven studied Seemi, sizing him up. It leaned its head slowly from one side to the other.

From across the room, No Face leaned forward to get a better look. The raven turned and followed the slave boy's movements.

Seemi said, "I want it to hop around."

Spirit Singer looked sternly at his nephew and said, "I told you this is serious. Do not ask it to do tricks. Ask it for what it knows."

Across the room, No Face closed his eyes.

Spirit Singer watched Seemi's progress. He glanced over at No Face and down at the raven. Their eyes, both tightly closed.

Chapter Nine

Seemi seemed frustrated and said, "It's going to sleep." Seemi waved his hands at the bird and the raven panicked. It flew directly at Seemi's face, as if to attack him. Seemi protected his face with one hand while swatting at the bird with his other hand. The raven flew around inside the rafters of the lodge, circling the room several times before turning and suddenly landing on No Face's shoulder.

Seemi was still unsettled and he looked at the bird cautiously.

Spirit Singer walked slowly to the door and opened it.

No Face then walked to the doorway, and the raven flew off into the air.

No Face stepped back inside the lodge and Spirit Singer closed the door after him.

Spirit Singer shook his head, smiled and then spoke, "In this world, the dream world, when you wear your mask that represents your animal and dance it, the real you from the spirit world becomes the dancer."

Seemi was confused. Nothing he heard or saw made sense.

Spirit Singer asked him, "Do you understand why I'm telling you these things?"

Seemi nodded and said, "When you dance the mask, you are somebody else."

"No." Spirit Singer shook his head. "You must dream the dream of your own animal. That is the first step." Spirit Singer reached into his supplies and placed a large chunk of wood in front of Seemi. He also deposited some crude stone carving tools on the ground. "Your mask, that is what you must carve. Every warrior must carve his own mask."

Seemi examined the block of wood and then took the tools into his hand.

No Face watched as Seemi fumbled with the carving tools.

Spirit Singer stepped to the door and opened it, saying, "Chief Sagawan's lodge is where I will be. We will be planning the winter celebration, where you will dance your mask. So work on it tonight, until you finish." Spirit Singer left the lodge, and Seemi instantly jumped to his feet.

He ran to the door and cracked it to watch as Spirit Singer walked away towards the chief's lodge. Seemi then hurried to No Face, and pointed down at the block of wood. "Get down there and carve me a mask," he commanded.

No Face responded, "Each one must carve their own. That is what the Circle of Feathers instructed."

"Did I ask for your opinion, slave? Now get down there and do as I say."

No Face dropped to the floor, took the block of wood, and picked up the tools. He began carving, digging small pieces of wood from one side of the block.

Chapter Ten
Spirit Singer Shares his Doubts about Seemi

Chief Sagawan

Spirit Singer sat next to Chief Sagawan on the raised platform. They ate together from the same tray of food. "Chief Sagawan, concern is what I have for my nephew Seemi," the shaman confided.

"Why should the great Circle of feathers have this concern?" The chief asked.

"The spirit, it does not move in him," was the answer.

Chief Sagawan paused and continued eating, then replied, "Perhaps the spirit is waiting until he has the wisdom of more years."

"It may never come. That is what I think," the shaman replied.

Chief Sagawan spoke with authority, "Then you must teach him. He must learn. These are things that you must do."

Spirit Singer hesitated, and then said, "What if you selected someone with remarkable talents?"

"Who could be such a person?" The chief asked.

"No Face, Seemi's slave," was the answer.

Chief Sagawan seemed shocked. He threw down his food as if it had suddenly gone bad. He frowned with displeasure and said, "How could this be, that the great Circle of Feathers would tell me such a thing? You must prepare Seemi. That is the way it has been. That is the way it will be!"

Back in Spirit Singer's lodge, No Face had made good progress, carving the mask of a bear. Seemi stepped over to look. He examined the mask and frowned, saying, "This looks more like a wolf or something." He threw the half-finished mask on the ground and complained, "Why couldn't you do a better job? Now I'll have to do it myself."

Seemi scavenged through his uncle's belongings until he found another block of wood. No Face picked up the discarded mask and held it up carefully, examining it.

Seemi looked at No Face and said, "You take that thing somewhere in the forest and bury it so my uncle won't find it."

No Face clutched the stone carving tools and stepped toward the door with the mask.

Seemi called after him, "And don't bother coming back inside tonight. You will sleep outside with the bears until you learn how to please me better." No Face nodded and smiled as he exited the lodge.

No Face and the Bear Mask.

From a mountain ledge, overlooking the village below, No Face sat beneath a tree. He used the stone carving tool he had taken from Spirit Singer's lodge. As he worked on the bear mask, he heard magical sounds coming from the slopes of Elos Mountain. There were animal cries, whispers, and human laughter. He also heard a distant chant and drumming. No Face looked around, but he saw nothing but the burnt out mountainside below him. He returned to his carving.

The lingering twilight revealed that there had been progress on the mask. The block of wood had become the excellent likeness of a bear. The sounds around him continued as he worked. As he rubbed vigorously on the mask, the chanting and drumming increased. Suddenly there was a flash of light. No Face found himself transported into a dreamlike state. He looked up suddenly into broad daylight. The sun was beating down. He stared into the bright light. He looked around and realized that he was sitting in the middle of the Mayukett village of his birth. When he turned back, he saw his mother and father standing before him.

His father asked, "Are you ready, son?" No Face joined his father, then answered, "Yes, I'm ready, father." The father and son departed for the canoes at the beach with the other men from the tribe. No Face turned and waved to his mother and then climbed into a canoe with his father, who looked at him proudly and said, "Today my son, you will become a Mayukett whale hunter."

No Face sat near the rear of the Canoe.

Three large 25-foot canoes dashed through the ocean waves, pushed forward by two sails and the six paddlers on each side. No Face sat near the rear of the canoe. The knot of fear in the pit of his stomach reminded the boy that today was the beginning of a new chapter in his life. He looked back at his father, who was sitting in the last seat, steering with his paddle, and asked, "Chief Wocash will certainly find us a whale, don't you think father?"

His father laughed a hearty laugh and said, "Knowing this is your first whale hunt, I'm sure he will find us one, perhaps two."

In the distance the coastline faded away. The canoes moved deeper into the open ocean. The swells became larger, tossing the canoes like bobbing driftwood. No Face clung fiercely to the side of the boat. In between swells, everyone paddled vigorously as the boats were steered through the crashing waves.

The Mayukett shaman, wearing a bird mask, with his outstretched arms covered with feathers, stood at the front of the boat. He waved his arms as if he were flying over the sea. As the birdman looked out at the horizon, he suddenly cried, "Whale! Whale!"

The rhythm of the paddling increased dramatically, as everyone used every ounce of energy left. No Face watched as they descended upon the gracefully moving giant. Chief Wocash stood and readied his wood harpoon, with its sharpened mussel shell point. A small whale sinew rope was attached to the butt of the harpoon. That in turn connected to a larger cedar rope coiled on the floor of the canoe. A series of 20 sealskin floats lay neatly tucked under the first few seat planks. As the canoe neared the immense mammal, the whale raised its back out of the water, presenting an inviting target. The chief lifted the harpoon and plunged it deeply into the body of the giant animal.

No Face grimaced when he saw the enormous amount of blood that gushed from the wound. The whale snapped its tail and dove beneath the surface. The rope began to uncoil as it followed the whale in the depths. The sealskin floats, which were spaced along the rope, were dragged one-by-one into the water. Each float skimmed the surface of the water for a few moments before disappearing under the wake of the canoe. When the last float left the boat, the rope snapped tight and the boat lurched forward, pulled through the water by the wounded whale. The speed of the boat and the great waves, churned by the ocean, battered the warriors, who clung to the side of the canoe. Suddenly the canoe came to a complete stop.

The birdman at the front of the boat watched as the rope angled down, then turned to the chief and said. "He's sounding." As the whale dove deep, the angle of the rope was almost straight down.

We'd better cut the rope before he pulls us under." The Birdman observed. Chief Wocash stepped forward to examine the rope. He grabbed it and pulled to test its tautness. To his surprise, the rope pulled easily from the water. A look of bewilderment crossed the chief's face as one of the sealskin floats popped up to the surface right next to the canoe. Every eye in the canoe focused on that float, as another one popped into view on the other side of the canoe. Every head in the boat turned in unison. There was total silence as a third float, then a fourth, and a fifth all appeared at various places around the canoe. Immediately after the sixth float appeared next to No Face and his father at the rear of the canoe, the entire craft trembled violently and then lifted into the air. No Face looked down as the water receded below them. He leaned over the edge and caught a glimpse of the whale's enormous eye directly below him.

There was a cracking; splintering sound as the boat came apart, separating the bow from the stern. The broken stern section flipped up into the air and turned upside down, spilling all the occupants into the water. He struggled to the surface and managed to gasp a few breaths before another large wave took him under. When he could catch his next breath, No Face reached out and grabbed one of the seating planks from the wrecked canoe. He positioned himself on the plank in an effort to stay above the water. He looked in every direction for the other canoes in their party, but he could not see anyone. He began to paddle while clinging to the buoyant wood. After a few minutes, No Face stopped swimming and looked around. A large wave washed over him and he had to scramble to keep ahold of the plank. He, once again, positioned the piece of wood under him and continued paddling. No Face, exhausted after several hours, clung tightly to the wooden plank as night closed in. The water was bitterly cold and he shivered uncontrollably. He tried his best to stay conscious. He would swim a few strokes then stop, then swim a few more strokes and stop.

No Face awakened on a beach with dark volcanic sand. He heard voices and someone poked him. He looked up to see several young Kiltook boys laughing at him. One of them was Seemi.

Seemi looked down and saw the boy's face, completely caked with sand. "Hey look," he cried. "He doesn't have a face." Seemi laughed and all the other boy's joined him, pointing and jeering.

The boy with no face.

Chapter Eleven
The Vision Ends

Back on the bluff above the Kiltook village, the vision ended. A bird's song awoke No Face to his painful reality. He looked around and realized it was morning. A ray of sunshine bathed the ground around him. He looked down and saw the completed bear mask glowing in the sunlight. No Face picked up the mask, admired it for a moment, then stood and carried it to a cleft in the rocks. He hid the mask and covered it with moss and tree branches. The boy stood and started back towards the village, but an outstretched hand grabbed his shoulder and stopped him. No Face turned quickly and found Spirit Singer looking down at him quietly. "I slept and dreamed with the animals, as Seemi commanded," No Face explained.

Talk is what we must do.

Chapter Eleven

"Sleeping, that is what I was doing too," the shaman answered. "Then I had a dream that you were up here." Spirit Singer took a seat on the ground and motioned for No Face to join him, then said, "Talk, is what we must do."

No Face sat down and looked cautiously at the shaman as Spirit Singer continued, "In my dream there was something very strange indeed. You have learned from my example and my lessons, but Seemi has not. Someday you will be a great shaman. But Seemi will not. "No Face gazed into the shaman's eyes with understanding. Spirit Singer continued speaking, "The Circle of Feathers is what I wish you could wear for the Kiltook tribe. A choice, however, is something I do not have. Through the mother's side of the family, that is how the Kiltook people trace their descent. Although a father will love his own son, it is his sister's children, not his own, who will inherit his wealth and status."

No Face nodded in understanding, as Spirit Singer continued. "When my sister's son Seemi came to live in my lodge, he was 11. That is when my present turmoil began. Now he is 17 and his training is something I must complete. He will someday wear the Circle of Feathers. Discipline is something he does not have. It is something I blame solely on his father. Sloth begets sloth. The boy is living proof." No Face was amazed that the shaman would speak of Seemi so candidly. Absolutely nothing, that is what he has learned." Spirit Singer continued. "Avoiding work and making himself look good, these are his only talents."

Spirit Singer looked down sympathetically at No Face, then with sadness in his voice he said, "Great sorrow is what I have for my people." "Into the future is where I have looked, and the end approaches too swiftly. Seemi will not be prepared. No Face, your help is what I ask for. Your power, strength and courage, you must give to the Kiltook people."

No Face frowned at Spirit Singer's request. He looked deeply into the shaman's eyes and responded, "I too feel sorrow, but not for the Kiltook people."

"Tell me what you want." Spirit Singer asked.

"My heart longs to be with my people," was the reply.

Spirit Singer shook his head with disapproval. "If you left, which direction would you go? Would you go North, or South?"

"I would go in the direction that welcomes me," No Face answered.

"But if you don't know where you are going," the shaman stated. "How will you be able to find your way home?"

No Face replied, "I would let it find me."

"If your home were close, your father would surely have come looking for you," the shaman said with emphasis.

"My father's spirit mingles now with the Great Spirit. His comforting touch guides me everyday," said No Face.

Spirit Singer shook his head and said softly, "The impossible, that is what you wish for. Our people will need your power someday soon. You should give up these ideas of going home. You must stay with the Kiltook people and help us."

No Face looked out to the sea with longing. He did not respond.

While No Face stood on the bluff, lost in thought, Bear ambled through the forest, navigating with his remaining senses. Snake kept his eyes open for potential obstacles.

Bear and Snakey ambled through the forest.

61

Chapter Eleven

Snakey, having been lost in thought for some minutes, finally said what was on his mind, "So, let me get this straight. You, the blind bear, and me the crippled snake are going to bring back life to the destroyed forest. Is that the plan?"

"Yes," said Bear.

Snakey continued, "And please tell me again, why you feel so compelled to do this?"

"In Bear's dream, the great Cave Bear said to do it. He said if Bear did it, he would restore Bear's sight."

"Oh yes, the great Cave Bear in your dream. How exactly did he say to go about doing this?" Snakey asked.

Bear paused and then responded, "He didn't say how to do it. He just said to do it."

Snakey shook his head and asked, "Do you have a little idea or anything?"

"Bear thought we might start by just going to the living forest and talking with everyone we meet."

"Yes, I can see it now," the snake said sarcastically. "I'll say hello, Mr. and Mrs. Mouse. Would you mind moving back to the burned-out forest, so I can more easily catch you and eat you?"

Bear ignored Snakey's sarcasm as they entered a field with brilliant purple wild flowers. He sniffed a flower, heard a giggle and said, "Why don't we start with the plants?"

"It makes no difference to me," Snakey replied. "I'm just along for the ride on this little 'Life Quest' of yours." Bear lowered himself down on his belly among the freshness and beauty of the wild flowers. The petals tickled his nose, causing him to sneeze.

A chorus of tiny voices responded "Bless you."

The Legend of Elos Mountain

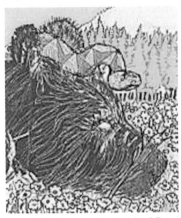

Bear and Snakey in the field of flowers.

Snakey looked around bewildered, asking, "Who said that?"

"We did," was the response. "We are the wild flowers. We're the spirit of giving."

Bear nuzzled another flower and got another tiny giggle in response. "We're on a quest," Bear explained. "We want to bring life back to the burned part of the forest. We need your help."

"We are not all just ornaments you know." The flower replied. "We are also food supply. Many of us have lessons to teach, like thorns and thistles. There are those among us who no one wants, like the weeds. They are merely misdirected flowers who have forgotten their calling."

"So you can help us?" Snakey asked.

"You must eat us," was the reply. "Then roll around among us to capture our seed and take us where we should go."

"Do what?" Snakey asked.

Bear instantly understood. He began to roll and frolic through the flowers. The snake hung on for dear life. Stopping periodically to eat various flowers. Bear tumbled through a thicket and collected a variety of briars and thistles to add to the wild assortment clinging to his thick coat.

Snakey's only comment was, "I sure hope you know what you're doing."

Bear gleefully plunged on. Soon, they found themselves in the middle of a field of fresh green grass. Bear flopped onto the ground and rolled through the soft carpet.

"Come lie with us and rest," said the grass.

"Who said that," Snakey demanded.

"It is us; we are the grasses of the field."

"Oh great", replied Snakey. "Now I'm talking to the grass."

"Rest with us before you move on," said the grass. "Lie down and take a nap with us. Let us comfort you and keep you warm."

Bear rolled onto his back and wallowed in the grass.

Deer Mask for the Fall Celebration.

The Legend of Elos Mountain

Back in the Village, all the families were getting ready for the fall celebration. In Spirit Singer's lodge, Seemi was dressed in his best ceremonial costume. He was wearing a leather coat decorated with beads. In his hands, he held an elaborately painted animal mask. It resembled Tamba.

Tamba

Seemi turned to No Face and barked an order, "Help me put this on." No Face helped Seemi with the mask, twisting it a bit to make it fit. Seemi turned toward Spirit Singer, who had not yet put on his mask and asked, "How do I look, uncle?"

Spirit Singer turned and said, "The bear in my dream, the one that attacked you, that is what you look like."

Seemi was surprised and reached up to lift the mask from his face, and asked, "You had a dream about my bear?"

"Yes," Spirit Singer replied. "Only in my dream there were two of them." Spirit Singer's revelation unnerved Seemi. He remained quiet, and lowered his mask over his face. He then turned and ran out of the lodge.

No Face began cleaning up after Seemi, who had left his regular clothes scattered about the lodge. Spirit Singer looked at the boy and said, "No Face, my mask, will you help me?" No Face stepped over and took the mask, positioning it carefully over the shaman's face. He then stepped back and looked at it carefully. It was the mask of a snake.

"Straight, is that the way it is? Asked Spirit Singer.

No Face looked at the mask from several angles and then nodded his approval.

"This is the mask I first danced when I was your age," Spirit Singer confided.

No Face looked down, lost in thought.

Spirit Singer continued speaking, "Since you are not a member of the tribe, you are not allowed to participate in these rituals. I am sorry. Watching from the door of the lodge is something you are welcome to do."

"Thank you," No Face replied.

Spirit Singer exited the lodge.

No Face stepped to the open door, and then closed it.

The fire in the center of the large stone circle seemed to dance and flicker to the beat of the throbbing drums. The rhythmic pulse moved through the masked tribesmen, causing them to move as one giant organism. Spirit Singer, in his snake's head mask stood before the fire with outstretched hands. The drums suddenly stopped as the shaman spoke.

"Great Spirit, live through us. From your mighty mountain top, come down and live through the Kiltook people."

The Legend of Elos Mountain

The drums erupted into a new complicated rhythm. Various masked dancers entered the stone circle and began to perform a ritual dance around the fire. Those who were standing outside the circle, waited for the spirit to move them. More people began joining the dance, as a few others began to leave the circle.

Spirit Singer focused his attention on the mask of a gray bear that had appeared at the edge of the stone circle.

It was No Face, wearing his bear mask. With a sudden leap, No Face entered the circle and joined the dancing animals. He jumped and rolled joyously on the ground. He tumbled and twisted as he chased the flames around the circle of fire. At one point, he fell on his back and wallowed through the dirt. He then leaped to his feet and raised arms into the air. As he raised his arms, there was the sound of a roaring bear.

Spirit Singer heard the sound and looked at the bear masked dancer with his arms raised. The dancer continued around the circle and then stopped and raised his arms again, Spirit Singer, once again, heard the roar of the mighty cave bear.

No Face looked out from inside the mask.

From inside the mask, No Face looked out at the maddening dancers. The fire seemed to spin past his view through the eyeholes of the mask. He came face to face with another dancer. It was Spirit Singer in his snake mask.

Chapter Eleven

They danced together for a short time and then moved away in opposite directions. The dancing feet kicked up dust, which combined with the smoke from the fire, obscured No Face's view, making it appear that he was running through the clouds. Suddenly a giant black thunderstorm appeared next to him. No Face peered into the inky blackness. Out of the storm came a voice, "I am nothing. I am nowhere. I was before creation. I am the source of all pain. I am here to help you remember why you are here. My lies and deceit will make truth hard to bare. I am darkness. I am fear. You must breathe in my air so you may know me." No Face breathed deeply as the storm began flashing with bolts of lightning and booming great claps of thunder. As he continued running, he moved past the thunderstorm and approached a large group of puffy white clouds. He heard a melodic voice say, "Come be part of us. We are everywhere. We are the before and the after. We are love and happiness. We are made of water, light and air. Let us show you who we are. Come in and breath our air. Come inside."

No Face turned and ran into the white fluff. Various shades of pink; orange; red; yellow; pale green and blue floated past like currents of energy. A figure stood in the center of the confusion of colors. The figure floated closer and materialized in the form of a tall Indian. No Face realized it was his father.

Suddenly the scene changed and No Face was once again around the fire. Through the smoke from the burning embers, the drums continued pounding their relentless tempo.

The Legend of Elos Mountain

Morning Star's Deer Mask.

Another dancer in a deer mask, approached No Face and began to dance with him. The bear and the deer danced their dance of life. The bear gave chase and caught her, running circles around the deer. The two of them suddenly stopped, turned and began running again, continuing the dance cycle once more. Finally, both were exhausted and left the stone circle to rest. They were both breathing heavily through the air holes in the nostrils of their masks.

Through her deer mask, Morning Star said, "Hello Bear."

Behind the bear mask, No Face said, "Hello deer."

"Do you think there will ever come a time when we can be friends?" The deer asked.

"Perhaps," the bear replied. "but only in the spirit world."

"But, not in this world? Not here?" The deer asked.

"You are a deer in this world. I am a bear. We do what we must do in this world."

"What if we could do anything we wanted in this world?" she asked.

"We can." The bear responded. "but we'll have to stop being a deer and a bear."

Seemi, wearing his elaborate bear mask, saw the bear and the deer together. He glanced back at Spirit Singer who raised his hands while standing next to the fire.

Chapter Eleven

The remaining dancers turned and left the circle and the drumming halted. Spirit Singer motioned to Seemi who stepped proudly into the circle. Pointing at Seemi in his mask that resembled Tamba, Spirit Singer cried, "Tomorrow, this great bear begins his walkabout. For seven days, that is how long he will live alone in the forest. He will communicate with the spirits. That is what he will do. He will ask for their guidance. That will be his quest." Spirit Singer lowered his hands and the drumming restarted.

Seemi began dancing alone. It was a choppy, clumsy dance consisting mainly of threatening gestures made by his hands, held in an imitation of claws.

High on a bluff overlooking the village, Tamba glared down at Seemi's dance and roared loudly.

Chapter Twelve
Bear and Snakey in the grassy field.

The field of grass.

Bear yawned widely as he woke up. He stretched and looked around. The two companions had slept all night in the field of grass.

Snakey shook his head to clear his brain and asked, "So what's the plan for today? We can talk to more flowers. I know! We can find some tasty veggies. Or maybe we could spend the day talking to bugs?"

Bear ignored his companion's snide tone and said, "Today we visit the trees, and anyone else we meet along the way."

"Oh great," Snakey replied. "We're going to talk to the trees. I hope none of my friends are around to see this." Bear stood and stretched, and then he meandered his way through the grassy field and into the trees.

As they entered the forest, Snakey looked up at the tall cedars, firs, oaks, aspens, and birches. They seemed to be waving their giant leafy branches to welcome the two travelers.

Chapter Twelve

Bear stopped and listened to the sound of the wind as it gently rustled the leaves. "Hello." Said Bear.

"Oh boy, here we go again," Snakey remarked.

"Hello?" Bear queried once more.

The wind carried a strange whispery voice that seemed to echo throughout the forest. It was the voice of the trees. "Why are you here?" asked the trees.

The eerie voice spooked the snake.

Bear looked around, as the sound appeared to be coming from every direction. He answered, "We are on a quest to bring life back to the burned part of the forest."

"What do you need?" asked the trees.

"We need you," answered Bear. "You are the trees, right?"

"Yes, we are the trees. We grow in a sacred circle, an everlasting spiral, and the cycle of life. Our greenery is our mark of beauty and grandeur. We produce food, provide shelter and share our secrets with the wind. We are the Children of the Wind. The cottonwoods are whispering old stories once again, while the Weeping Willows are watching down by the waterline. The only ones who listen are the children of the wind.

"We need to take you with us, but Bear is not sure how to…"

The answer came in a soft answering whisper, "Look within. Our lesson is seeking the spirit of creation. The path to understanding the truth. Everything that is from the spirit is true. We are strong, ageless, and confident. Learn from our leaves as they fall. Each one is unique. The colors within each are a lesson. Catch our leaves, eat our seeds and carry us with you."

The voice stopped and Bear continued to listen. A mighty wind blew through the forest and thousands of leaves rained down on Bear and Snakey.

Bear understood what they needed to do. He began to bite at the falling leaves. He chased them, rolling and scooping them up. Finding a pile of acorns and other nuts, he gorged himself until he could eat no more. With his belly full and his coat covered with clinging leaves and seeds, Bear began to waddle out of the forest.

As they rounded a large ancient oak, Snakey spotted two mice on the ground talking to each other.

"What is it?" Bear asked.

"Dinner," was the reply.

Bear sniffed and detected the small rodents. The two small creatures were deep in the middle of an argument and did not notice Bear and Snakey.

Mr. Mouse said accusingly, "I put those acorns around here somewhere and you obviously moved them."

Mrs. Mouse replied, "I didn't move them. You're always moving things and then you forget where you put them and you try and blame me for your mistakes."

Bear cocked his head and said to Snakey, "See if you can talk them into moving back to the burned-out forest. We need everyone we can get."

"You're kidding. You want me to talk to them?"

"Yes," Bear answered.

"But they look so tasty," Snakey pleaded.

"Now is not the time for that," Bear said firmly.

"Gees, I can't believe I'm doing this," the snake complained. Snakey extended himself away from Bear's neck and looked down at the mice, who were still bickering. Snakey shook his head, cleared his throat and said, "Excuse me Mr. and Mrs. Mouse, we're on a quest to…"

The two mice looked up and saw the enormous bear with the serpent around its neck. They shrieked in total panic and vanished out of sight before the snake could finish his sentence.

"Well, there goes dinner," was his final comment.

Chapter Twelve

Spirit Singer performed a ritual.

Back at the Kiltook village, Spirit Singer stood in the center of the common area, performing a ritual. He poured cornmeal from a bag, into a circle on the ground. He then stood in the middle of the circle, holding a feather in the air. A group of young village women, assembled around the cornmeal circle, listening intently as Spirit Singer spoke. "Your path is the link between you and the Great Spirit," he explained. "Seeing your path, that is what the Vision Feather will teach you. The one of you the feather chooses will receive the gift of vision.

A glimpse of the future will be the gift from the great creator." Spirit Singer tossed the Vision Feather into the air. It floated on the air current, dancing above the circle of women. Eventually, the feather came to rest in front of Morning Star. She reached down, picked up the feather and stepped into the cornmeal circle.

Morning Star was chosen by the Vision Feather.

Spirit Singer moved closer and helped Morning Star position the vision Feather, so that she held it at arm's length in front of her face.

The shaman spoke, "On the feather, that is what you must focus your attention. Balance your thoughts and feelings. Everyday thoughts, that is what you must clear from your mind. New images and sounds is what you will soon hear."

Morning Star obeyed. Soon, she could only hear her own breathing.

The other women in the circle began to spin around the edge of her peripheral vision as she focused on the feather. Soon the others were nothing but a blur of spinning light. Images and sounds began to emanate from the hurricane of color. There was an image of a knife and the Circle of Feathers. The bear mask that No Face wore for the ritual dance appeared and floated across her field of view.

Chapter Twelve

Abruptly, a charging black bear loomed above her. She was frightened, but she did not waiver.

Suddenly a gray bear with white glowing eyes and a serpent wrapped around its neck appeared. The bear was walking through a field of beautiful wild flowers.

Morning Star found herself standing in the field of wild flowers. She felt calm and happy. She caressed the flowers and smelled their sweet fragrance. The whirlwind of color slowed and came to an abrupt stop. Morning Star looked away from the Vision Feather and saw Spirit Singer's smile.

"A vision," said Spirit Singer. "That is what you had."

Morning Star felt overwhelmed. She could hardly speak. "Yes, a vision," she answered.

"Your path is what you saw," Spirit Singer continued.

"Yes, my path," she answered.

"Did you see a place?" the shaman asked.

She replied, "I saw the place."

Spirit Singer looked directly into her eyes and said, "That is where you must go, now!"

Morning Star gave the Vision Feather to Spirit Singer and then stepped out of the cornmeal circle. She turned and ran out of the village.

Spirit Singer examined the Vision Feather. He looked at it to see if there were any lingering images left. As he studied the feather, an image appeared. He saw Seemi walking through the ashes. Seemi walked alone in the burned-out forest on his walkabout. He saw two mice run past. He found the place where he had planned to camp, and looked around. He called out, "No Face, are you here yet?"

No Face emerged from a hiding spot carrying a large bundle, which he placed at Seemi's feet.

Seemi opened the bundle to find many comforts from home, including food; water; a mat to sleep on; bow and arrow, and a woven fabric to use as a makeshift tent. "Not a word to anyone about this," Seemi commanded. No Face nodded. "You can go," said Seemi, "but check back every day to see if I need anything.

Bear and Snakey at the Creek.

Bear and Snakey arrived at a small creek in the burned part of the forest. Snakey looked around and said, "Well, we're here. What do we do now?"

"What comes naturally," Bear replied, as he began to claw the earth out to form a small hole. He then squatted to relieve himself. "Oh My," said Snakey, his eyes wide as he saw what Bear was doing. He looked away and tucked his head down into Bear's fur.

When Bear was finished, he dug up more earth to cover the hole. Snakey looked up as they began moving. Suddenly, Bear began running, and then he slid and tumbled across the black charred ground. He deposited seeds, leaves, thorns, and thistles from his coat. Small plants began to sprout behind him almost immediately. Bear abruptly stopped and sniffed the air. He turned his head and sniffed.

"What is it?" asked Snakey. "Bear smells the bad human who ran away from our fight," was his reply.

Seemi relaxed on his sleeping mat under his makeshift tent. He was dozing off, when he was startled by the noise of a branch breaking. The boy jumped up, coming to full alert. He was stunned to see Spirit singer in his complete costume, wearing his snake mask.

Spirit Singer in his Snake Mask.

Seemi was too shocked to make sense of what was happening. "What are you doing here, Uncle?" he asked. Spirit Singer did not reply. Instead, he angrily grabbed the provisions and threw them in every direction, as far as he could. He poured the water out of its container and threw the food to the ground. He then stomped and ground it all into the earth and ashes. As a last gesture, he grabbed the tent and sleeping mat, tearing them into long strips. He then took the strips with him, walking away, dragging a colorful trail of fabric.

Seemi stood dumbfounded in the middle of the mess. Some distance away, No Face was walking through the forest on his way back to the village, after delivering the supplies to Seemi. The trail came to a vast field of wild flowers. As No Face looked out at the field, he saw someone standing in the middle of the glorious display of colors. It was Morning Star.

Morning Star in her Deer Mask.

She walked among the wild flowers, trying to understand the meaning of her vision. She looked up to see No Face standing before her.

Finally, No Face broke the awkward silence. "Hello, Morning Star," He said softly.

"Hello No Face," she answered.

"When I dream," said No Face. "I see a place where we could be friends."

"Perhaps," replied Morning Star, "but only in the spirit world. Not in this world."

"Why not this world," he asked. "It is the one where we are having this dream right now."

Morning Star looked at No Face and spoke gently, "because you are a slave, and I am the chief's daughter. We are different. We must do what we do, here in this world."

No Face smiled quizzically. "What if we could dream any dream we wanted, right here in this world?"

Morning Star then asked, "What would you do then?"

Chapter Twelve

No Face responded, "I would leave, and I would take you with me. We would go to a place where a bear and a deer could live together in happiness."

Morning Star looked at No Face and smiled. She looked down as she twirled a yellow flower between her flattened hands. Then she spoke, " I thought that was you in the bear mask. You know that if you had been caught, they would probably have killed you?"

"That was the spirit world. There are no rules there."

"But there are rules here and the penalties are real," she stated firmly.

"Fear is not what I focus on," No Face answered. "I'm not afraid, are you?"

Deep in thought, Morning Star looked out over the field of flowers. Then she looked into his eyes and said, "Yes, I am afraid. I can't help it."

No Face reached down and took Morning Star's hand in his own.

She looked up into his eyes. "How is it that a deer and a bear could live together in this world?" she asked.

"Because of their love for one another," was his reply.

"How would they find this place where they could be together?" She asked.

"They would have to go through the spirit world to find it," he said.

Morning Star looked at the flower she was holding. The petals were all gone from the little yellow flower. She asked, "But what if they can't find their way back to this world? What would they do?"

No Face smiled and answered with conviction in his voice. "Then at least they would be together. And they could dream this life dream another time, with another mask."

A tear formed in Morning Star's eye.

No Face gently brushed it from her cheek.

The Legend of Elos Mountain

Some distance away, Spirit Singer stopped in the middle of the ash and debris in the desolated forest. He formed a circle of stones and then took the shredded cloth from Seemi's sleeping mat and began to tear it into long colorful pieces. He then arranged them on the ground. The design resembled the woven strands of a spider's web. Spirit Singer took one of the pieces of colorful cloth and began to roll it into a ball. He then took another piece of cloth, before he was finished with the first. After rolling it up for a few moments, he took a third piece. He was making a multi-colored prayer tie.

As Spirit Singer worked, Bear and Snakey walked past him in the distance.

Snake noticed the shaman, but the shaman did not see them.

After he finished rolling all the pieces of cloth into the ball, the shaman stopped and dug a hole, using a stone. He put the cloth ball into the hole and buried it.

Spirit Singer stood up and walked away. A beautiful green plant emerged up through the soil and ash that covered the hole. It grew rapidly and spread its branches, becoming a full and leafy elm tree. The buds began appearing everywhere, all around the tree. Then all in unison, the buds became a bouquet of brilliant wild flowers.

The wild flowers were identical to the flowers in the field where Morning Star and No Face were lying together on their backs. There was a burst of color and fragrant smells. They held hands as they looked up at the sky and clouds.

Morning Star dropped No Face's hand and leaped to her feet. She smiled at him mischievously and started running. No Face got up and began chasing her. Together they ran through the flowers, repeating the movements of their mask dance from the night before.

Meanwhile, Seemi walked alone in the forest. He came to an overlook and saw all the flowers below. He saw two people running and playing in the field of wild flowers. He recognized Morning Star and No Face and could not believe what he was seeing. Seemi picked up a rock and threw it at them. Then he ducked down out of sight. The rock landed a few feet from No Face and Morning Star. They stopped and looked around, and then they turned and ran for the cover of the forest.

Chapter Thirteen
The Mayukett People

Two strange canoes entered Elos Bay.

The Kiltook village was excited as two strange canoes entered Elos Bay. Chief Sagawan and Spirit Singer walked together with great dignity to the waters edge. Other villagers climbed upon the roofs of their lodges and began drumming on the wood planks, whooping, and yelling in excitement. The two canoes moved slowly towards the village. Each canoe was carrying five men, along with many bundles of provisions. The canoes nosed into the beach at last. As the men stepped out onto the land, a contingent of Kiltook warriors assembled in front of them carrying spears. The men from the canoes held their spears above their heads and chanted in unison. The Kiltook warriors did likewise, both groups chanting and dancing in a ritualized war greeting. The ritual came to a stop and Chief Sagawan raised his left arm in salute and said, "Welcome. We are the Kiltook people. We offer greetings and our friendship."

Azart of the Mayukett
people in his otter skin hat.

One of the men from the canoe stepped forward. He said, "My name is Azart. We bring you greetings from the Mayukett people. We have come to trade otter skins for food and provisions. We ask the great leader of the Kiltook people to allow us to rest here for three days, and then we will depart for our home.

Chief Sagawan paused only a moment before replying, "The Kiltook people welcome you. We shall share our food. You and your people shall be guests in my lodge. We will eat together and we will talk of the ocean and mountains that separate our two peoples." Azart returned to one of the canoes and retrieved an otter skin. Azart held the skin in the air, so the chief could see it. He then stepped over to Chief Sagawan, saying, "For honoring us with your welcome, I give you this as a sign of our thanks." Azart handed the skin to the chief who examined it and nodded his head in approval, saying, "It is good."

No Face and Morning Star arrived at the village and separated. Morning Star took her place behind her father.

No Face looked carefully at the visitors. They seemed familiar to him.

Chief Sagawan motioned for Azart and his men to follow him back to his lodge, saying, "Come! We will celebrate your journey."

Suddenly No Face recognized several of the men. These were people from his home village. He was openly excited with a tremendous smile on his face. As the men walked past, No Face barged through the crowd and grabbed Azart by the arm. The boy's sudden touch shocked Azart. He pushed him away. "You've come to rescue me. I knew you would." Azart looked confused. Chief Sagawan was angry and said, "This is not your place, slave! What is the meaning of your words?"

"I am Mayukett. These are my people," No Face cried out in anguish.

Azart cried, "Who are you?"

No Face replied, "I am White Bear, son of Rain Dancer. A whale destroyed our canoe. These people found me when I washed up on the beach, and rather than welcome me as a visitor from another tribe, they made me a slave and imprisoned me."

"Yes, I know the story of how the great whale destroyed Chief Wocash's canoe. The chief and seven men were saved."

"Tell me of my father, Dancing Rain?" No Face pleaded.

"He was not found," Azart replied.

No Face looked down and fought back the sadness.

"I'm sorry," said Azart, patting the boy on the back.

Chief Sagawan looked at Spirit Singer and then shrugged his shoulders. The chief then turned and continued walking toward his lodge.

There was a great celebration inside the chief's lodge. The chief and his family sat together on the left side of the raised platform, along with the senior elders of the village.

The Mayukett warriors sat together in a group on the right side of the platform, a place of honor.

A group of drummers played in one corner of the lodge, as Spirit Singer danced around the guests, performing a welcoming ritual. He sprinkled cornmeal and shook a rattle to purify the food that was cooking over the fire, as well as all around the perimeter of the fire pit. Boiling clay pots filled with fish and vegetables caused a steamy vapor to float around Spirit Singer as he danced.

When he finished the ritual, he turned to Azart and presented him with the gift of a pipe. "I give this to the warriors of the Mayukett on behalf of the Kiltook people." Azart took the pipe, as Spirit Singer removed a small burning stick from the fire. Spirit Singer lit the pipe as Azart took a long draw and then exhaled the smoke. He nodded and said, "It is good." Spirit Singer then took his place next to Chief Sagawan. The women began filling wooden platters with food. They carried platters of food to the chief. Next, they brought the same thing for the senior elders.

No Face carried a platter of boiled fish to the visitors. He placed the food in front of the warriors and they all began picking the food with their fingers, grabbing fingers full and stuffing them into their mouths hungrily. No Face stood admiring Azart, who took another mouthful of fish and noticed No Face looking at him. No Face put another platter in front of Azart and in a low quiet voice, he asked, "Please take me home."

Azart and his warriors talked in low tones among themselves. Azart asked, "What can we do?" A warrior named Watash, said, "When we leave, we'll hide him in the canoe."

Chapter Thirteen

Azart rejected the idea and shook his head disapprovingly. "No" he said. If we just take him, there will be trouble. We will have to buy him. He is the son of Rain Dancer who is dead. We must buy his freedom and return him to the tribe and to his clan.

Azart looked at No Face for his reaction. No Face responded, "I think something can be worked out." No Face then looked across the room at Spirit Singer, sitting next to the chief. The two were talking in low tones and occasionally glancing at the Mayukett warriors.

The following morning as Spirit Singer was dressing; No Face entered his sleeping area. Spirit Singer looked over at the boy reluctantly. "What is it?" The shaman asked. "The Mayukett want me to return with them," he said. "Since my father's death, I'm the head of my clan. I must return." "Yes, I can see that you should go." Spirit Singer shook his head and sighed loudly, then continued. "Staying with us, that is what I had hoped. You are such a bright spirit. You could have helped out people in so many ways."

"You said that one day; I would be a great shaman. I know that is true. But when it happens, I will be a Mayukett shaman, not a Kiltook slave." Spirit Singer nodded his understanding and tried to calm the boy. He walked over, put his arm around No Face, and said, "I understand. Standing in your way, that is something I will not do."

No Face turned and stared deeply into Spirit Singer's eyes. "The Mayukett will buy my freedom. They want to do things the right way."

"That is good," Spirit Singer replied.

"Perhaps you could talk with Chief Sagawan and get his blessing." Suggested No Face.

Spirit Singer nodded and replied, "Speaking with Chief Sagawan, that is something I will do. Since Seemi found you on the beach, you belong to him." Spirit Singer saw that his statement made No Face visibly uneasy. He continued, "But, the chief's decision is what I will make sure Seemi accepts. Sorrow is what I will feel when you leave, No Face.

No Face smiled, feeling lifted by Spirit Singer's words. Spirit Singer started for the door, but then stopped suddenly and turned back to No Face and said, "I'm proud to have known you White Bear, son of Dancing Rain."

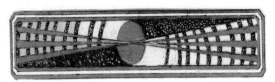

Chapter Fourteen
The Birds and the Bugs

Bear and Snakey were back in the old growth forest and addressing a flock of birds and a gathering of bugs and other crawling creatures. Bear was finishing his speech to the birds. "So we need you to fly back to the burned out forest. Anywhere you see new trees and bushes springing up, make nests and raise your young. The spirit of the mountain and my ancestor, the mighty cave bear have declared that if you believe and follow these instructions, it will be so. The forest will return, even fuller and more plentiful than before."

Snakey popped his head out from Bear's neck fur, startling the birds. He added, "And make sure you leave a few eggs lying around for me." The snakes comment greatly disturbed the birds.

"Don't pay any attention to him. He is just joking," said Bear, trying to sound lighthearted. Then Bear leaned down to address the tiny ant village, grasshopper corps, and centipede rows that had assembled. "And you my little friends. As many of you who will, must come back too."

One of the ants raised a tiny leg to get Bear's attention and asked. "How do we find this place?"

The Legend of Elos Mountain

"Bear will lead you," the grizzly answered. "Follow me." Bear and Snakey slowly walked off as the birds took to the air and formed a large formation before flying away.

Behind Bear and Snakey, a tiny caravan of creatures followed along. The contingent passed through fields of grass and fields of flowers. They moved down forest trails and eventually they came to the edge of a deep gorge. A dead tree had fallen across the gorge creating a bridge.

As Bear and Snakey arrived at the bridge, Snakey eyed it cautiously and said, "You better stop. There is a deep gorge ahead."

Bear stopped. He could smell the gorge.

"There's a tree bridge" Snakey explained. "But I'm not sure you can balance on it without being able to see."

"How do we get across?" Bear asked.

"You could jump," Snakey replied.

"Can Bear make it?" The grizzly wanted to know.

Snakey gauged the width of the gorge. He thought a moment and then said, "Yeah, I'd say we have a pretty good chance of making it."

"A pretty good chance?" Bear asked in a worried tone.

"No, I mean a good chance. We'll make it, no problem." The snake amended.

"Okay, then let's go," said Bear. Bear sniffed to check the location of the insects that were following. His sniffing caused blasts of air, which almost sucked the ants into Bear's nose.

One ant, the one who had asked the question, had to hang onto a blade of grass to keep from flying up Bear's nose. "Help, help," the ant cried.

Bear stopped sniffing and said, "You can use the tree bridge. Bear is going to jump."

Chapter Fourteen

The insects began marching over the tree bridge and assembling on the other side.

Bear moved back to get a running start. "You ready?" asked Bear.

"As ready as I'll get," Snakey answered.

Bear began to run as fast as he could towards the ledge.

At that moment, Snakey yelled, "Get Ready."

"How far?" asked Bear.

"Really far," cried Snake.

Bear jumped and flew through the air, out over the gorge. His landing was not graceful. He smashed into the wall below the ledge on the other side. Just his two front paws were clinging to the ledge above. Bear hung there a moment to catch his breath, then stated, "Next time, I'd like you to tell me when it's really, really far." Bear clawed and pulled with all his might, grinding his teeth as he slowly managed to pull himself and the snake to safety.

"See," said Snakey. "I said you'd make it. No problem."

Bear and Snakey continued their journey. The tiny universe of creatures followed them close behind.

Spirit Singer and the talking stick.

The Legend of Elos Mountain

Back in Chief Sagawan's lodge, Spirit Singer stood with the talking stick. The chief, the Tyee elders and the chief's family all listened to Spirit Singer speak. "The wisdom to decide what is right, that is what the Great Spirit gives to Chief Sagawan.

The chief nodded his approval. Spirit Singer continued, "The Mayukett, they are the traders who visit our village. There is a Mayukett among us. It is the slave No Face."

Sitting by her father, Morning Star listened attentively. There was a brief commotion. Short comments were exchanged between the elders and Chief Sagawan.

The chief raised his hand to silence the group so Spirit Singer could continue.

"The Mayukett would like to buy the slave, No Face, and take him home. They say he is the son of one of their elders, who is dead. He is entitled to the position his father held as head of their clan."

Chief Sagawan thought about it for a moment, and then he looked to Spirit Singer and asked, "What do you say on this, Spirit Singer who wears our Circle of Feathers?"

Letting the boy go, that is what we should do," answered the shaman.

The chief discussed the situation with the elders. After a few minutes, the discussion died down and the chief raised his arm and asked, "This slave boy, he should be the same one who started the fire?"

"Yes, replied Spirit Singer, "but it was an accident."

Chief Sagawan said firmly, "But much damage was done. Food and firewood were lost. I will allow the Mayukett to purchase the slave's freedom, but a price must be paid in compensation for the damage."

Morning Star looked to Spirit Singer to tell the truth about the fire. When she heard the truth hidden, she stood and addressed her father. "No Face is innocent. I saw Seemi start the fire and blame it on his slave."

Chapter Fourteen

Chief Sagawan glared at his daughter and said, "Sit down girl. You know better than to speak to me like this. You bring shame on us."

Morning Star's mother took her by the arm and led her outside.

The elders grumbled about Morning Star's outburst.

Chief Sagawan raised his hand to quiet the group. He spoke to Spirit Singer, "The slave No Face, he should belong to your nephew Seemi, yes?"

"Yes, he is the one who found him," Spirit Singer answered.

"Then Seemi, he should decide the price when he returns from his walkabout in two days. Spirit Singer bowed to the chief to show his respect.

Outside the chief's lodge, No Face stood watching Morning Star as she stood with her mother at the community fire. No Face was waiting for Spirit Singer to return.

Spirit Singer exited the chief's lodge and walked over to No Face.

No Face stood and eagerly awaited the news.

"You will have your freedom, that is what Chief Sagawan said to me," said the shaman.

No Face jumped into the air and yelled with joy, crying, "From this dream I will wake and never dream of this, ever again."

Spirit Singer added, "I will handle Seemi, so that the trade can be made for a token."

"What price will Seemi ask for me?" he asked.

"I have thought about this," admitted Spirit Singer. "For Seemi, it must be something with great power."

No Face seemed perplexed, saying, "All my people have are the otter skins they offer in trade for food.

Spirit Singer answered, "Your mask is what will be offered in trade."

The revelation shocked No Face. The shaman knew about his mask, and he questioned him, to make sure. "The mask?" he asked.

"Yes the mask," the shaman replied. "It has been danced and holds great power. That is what your people will say, and it will be the truth."

The prospect of giving away his beloved mask troubled the boy. He remembered the bitter cold night with no blanket. He remembered how his hands hurt from the cold as he chipped away at the mask while huddling near to his small fire on the bluff above the village. How did you know about my mask?" he asked.

"How could I not know," Spirit Singer answered. "You have great power No Face. I could see your spirit when you danced. You will offer the mask in trade to Seemi."

No Face thought about it for a time and then asked, "Is the mask truly a worthy trade for my freedom?"

Spirit Singer smiled ruefully and said, "For Seemi, the idea of owning a mask with great power will be too much for him to turn down."

Inside Spirit Singer's lodge, No Face talked with the Mayukett warriors about the plan. He gave his bear mask to Azart, saying, "Offer this to Seemi when he returns in two days."

Azart took the mask and examined it carefully, as No Face continued speaking,

"Tell him it has been danced and that it has great power."

Azart looked puzzled and No Face went on talking. "I know this to be true, because I danced the mask myself and it took me to the thunderstorms and to the white clouds where I saw my father." Azart nodded in understanding.

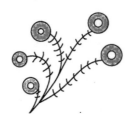

Chapter Fourteen

Then he responded, "We will use the mask to purchase your freedom. Then you will go home, where Chief Wocash will welcome you back with great warmth and dignity, as you will take your father's position as head of your clan."

No Face smiled and then began laughing.

Azart put his arm around the boy and they laughed together.

That night No Face could not sleep, for thinking about Morning Star. He finally gave up trying. He got up and snuck out of Spirit Singer's lodge and around behind the chief's lodge. He removed a wall plank and slithered through the opening. No Face crept to where Morning Star was sleeping and gently woke her up, putting his hand gently over her mouth to keep her from making a noise.

When Morning Star was awake and realized what was happening, she followed No Face back out of the lodge, through the small hole in the wall. The two of them ran together into the tree line above the village, where new growth bushes, grass and trees seemed to have appeared almost overnight. Once into the tree line, the two stopped.

No Face took both of Morning Star's hands in his own and said, "Soon, I will be leaving the Kiltook people."

"I know," she said, "I heard Spirit Singer talk with my father. He wants your people to pay for your freedom because he still thinks you started that fire. I tried to explain it to him, but he would not listen. He is so stubborn and blind to anything that threatens his perfect order.

No Face studied Morning Star's eyes. "Your eyes are so beautiful when you are angry. That you tried to help me means more than anything."

"Well, it did no good. It didn't help," she complained.

"Have no worries," he said reassuringly. "An arrangement has been made. When Seemi returns, the trade of a mask will be the cost of my freedom."

The thought saddened Morning Star. "I'll never see you again," she said.

"That is only if we are apart. But not if we are together," he replied, almost in a whisper.

Morning Star shook her head, "That is a foolish idea. I cannot go with you. I can't."

"You think that way now, but tonight, think of something else. Think of hiding aboard the canoe. Then tomorrow we will leave together," he said reassuringly.

"And when they find me missing," she said with conviction. "My father would send canoes after you. His warriors would attack and kill you. Forget it No Face. It is absolutely not possible." She turned and ran back to the edge of the forest. She stopped and looked back for one last comment. She said, "Goodbye, No Face. My heart will go with you." Morning Star ran back to the lodge and climbed through the hole in the wall.

Chapter Fifteen
No Face has his second Whale Hunt

Spirit Singer said,"No Face, ride with me on this Whale Hunt."

The following morning, the village people were conducting their routine affairs, when a single drum began beating in the common area. People began to emerge from their lodges, looking around for the meaning of the drum call. Chief Sagawan appeared at his doorway, as did Spirit Singer in the next lodge.

A scout appeared at Chief Sagawan's door crying, "Whales! It's an entire pod!"

Everyone sprang into action, bolting back inside his or her lodges to get ready for the hunt.

Back in his own lodge, Spirit Singer got quickly dressed in his ceremonial costume, including bands of eagle feathers.

No Face helped him dress, and then positioned the snake mask and the wing-like arm bands that made him appear half snake and half bird.

Spirit Singer stepped outside and began walking towards the beach.

No Face stood in the doorway watching him go.

Suddenly Spirit Singer stopped. He turned back to No Face and motioned for the boy to follow.

No Face ran and caught up with the shaman.

Spirit Singer said, "Since Seemi is not here, ride with me on this hunt."

No Face felt his chest tighten and a cold sweat broke out on his forehead. He knew he had to comply, if for no reason other than the need to conquer his fear of the destruction the whale had brought on his life, when it had destroyed their canoe. No Face tried to shut his mind off as he woodenly followed Spirit Singer to the canoe, where he took a seat behind Spirit Singer who sat in the bow of the canoe, as the warriors pushed off from the shore.

As they began paddling and picked up speed, they quickly cleared the bay and the inlet and began to ply the open ocean.

Now standing in the front of Chief Sagawan's canoe, Spirit Singer spread his winged arms as they flew over the water. Spirit Singer spotted the white geyser from a whale several hundred yards ahead and shouted, "Whale," Spirit Singer pointed and used his winged arm like a compass to direct the canoes in the right direction.

No Face looked at the white blast of water and air spewing from the whale. All the men were paddling furiously as a second and a third whale blow appeared. It was a family of large blue whales; an enormous bull, followed by his mate and a single offspring. Their back and tail emerged from the water and gracefully waved through the air in unison.

As the canoes neared the whales, Chief Sagawan stood and readied his harpoon. The canoe pulled along-side the female. Chief Sagawan thrust his harpoon deep into the animal's back. No Face grimaced and looked away.

The whale dove and the long rope attached to the harpoon began to uncoil over the side of the canoe. The sealskin floats few from the front of the canoe, one after another. The floats rode along the surface of the water, spaced twenty feet apart. After the last of the 20 floats had left the boat, the rope snapped tight and the canoe jerked forward, dragged by the wounded female. Spirit Singer watched the condition of the rope and floats carefully. He watched as the first of the floats in the distance began to submerge. One-by-one, the floats disappeared under the waves. The rope began to angle down, and the canoe began to slow.

Chief Sagawan joined Spirit Singer in the bow to examine the rope. A look of concern crossed the chief's face as he saw the angle of the rope continue to plummet. As a precaution, Chief Sagawan pulled a knife from his belt and prepared to cut the rope. However, before he could make his decision, the angle suddenly diminished. In the distance, the sealskin floats reemerged from the depths. Within a few moments more floats appeared, until all 20 were visible.

Then ahead, in the distance, the whale reappeared and blew a fountain of bloody froth from her blowhole. Chief Sagawan signaled to the other canoes and they moved in quickly for the kill. A second canoe overtook the whale and one of the elders in the front, jabbed a second harpoon into the animal, as more rope and sealskin floats shot out of the canoe.

Moments later, the third and fourth canoes converged on the wounded animal and thrust their harpoons into the dying beast. The whale tried valiantly to pull all four boats and their floats, but it slowly weakened and gave up the fight. The whale rolled over, revealing her white underbelly. There was great celebrating in all of the canoes. Everyone was cheering except No Face who felt sorrow, like a giant fist in his belly. Several men dove overboard and began rigging the ropes and floats to transport their prize back to the village.

The Legend of Elos Mountain

Morning Star was the first to see the canoes.

Looking out over Elos Bay, Morning Star was first to see the arrival of the canoes.

All four boats were paddling vigorously, pulling the whale by the tail, as it floated limply behind them, aided by twenty or more sealskin floats on each side. The remaining villagers either scrambled to the beach, or climbed to the roofs of their lodge and began drumming on the planks. When the canoes reached the beach, the villagers took the ropes and helped pull their prize catch onto the sand.

No Face stepped away from the canoe and walked solemnly away.

He passed Morning Star who stopped to talk to him. He did not say anything to her.

She noticed a tear running down his cheek.

Chapter Fifteen

New growth will spring up everywhere.

Back in the burned part of the forest, Bear and Snakey were directing traffic. They were sending tiny convoys of creatures in every direction, dispersing them throughout the burned area, which was sprouting new growth as they worked.

Snakey was giving orders like a natural leader. "Hey you grasshoppers, you're going the wrong way, You ants, follow the rest." "Just let them go where they want," Bear cautioned him. "But they're all bunching up. We've got too many ants in one place and all the grasshoppers and centipedes want to hang out together," Snakey complained. A flock of birds flew overhead. Snakey looked up and admired their perfect formation.

Bear smelled something and began twisting his head to determine the direction of the odor.

"What is it?" asked Snakey.

It's Tamba, he is close.

"Bear smells Tamba, He is close." Bear pointed his nose and said, "That way."

Snakey looked in the direction Bear was pointing, but could not see anything. He said, "I think we're finished here with these little-folk. They can figure things out for themselves. What do you say we head back and talk with the deer, or the coyotes? We need to see the ones we haven't talked to yet."

Bear replied, "The larger animals will return in the spring." He continued to sniff.

Snakey was vividly worried. "Listen," said Snakey. "I know you are truly one of the bravest bears in the forest. But you are not ready to take on Tamba in your present condition."

"Bear didn't do too badly last time. If he comes, Bear will stand and fight." Was the reply.

"Ah, if you'll recall, um, without the help of that human, you might not be here at all," Snakey reminded him.

Bear hesitated a moment, then said, "Bear would have beaten Tamba anyway."

"Oh sure, said Snakey. "Tamba had separated us, and he was going for your throat, when the boy stepped in."

Bear felt a sudden chill run down his back as he remembered, then he answered, "Nevertheless, Bear will never run from a fight."

Chapter Fifteen

"Never?" asked Snakey, as he looked up to see Tamba charging them from over a ridge. "There's always a first time."

Bear caught Tamba's smell, as Snakey continued," your old friend Tamba is charging straight at us."

Bear vacillated, unable to decide what to do.

Snakey asked, "Well, what's it going to be?"

Bear turned quickly and started running away from Tamba. "Bear will run," he said.

Snakey sighed and said, "I think that is the wisest thing I've ever heard you say. "That way," said the snake with a shake of his rattle."

Bear ran as quickly as he could, saying, "Bear will fight Tamba another day, when Bear's eyes have healed."

Snakey hung on tight, looking ahead, surveying their path. Then he responded, "Sounds like a very good plan to me."

Then Bear added, "Um, Don't tell anyone about this. Okay?"

"Your secret is safe with me," was the reply. "Oh by the way, go a little this way," he said with one hiss. There is a gorge ahead." Bear angled right and increased his speed as he heard Tamba breathing hard and closing the gap between them.

Snakey's voice carried urgency as he cried, "Get ready to jump. It's…"

Bear cut him of, saying, "Bear knows… really, really far."

"Jump now Bear!"

Bear leaped with all his strength and glided gracefully

through the air over the precipice. This time, they landed squarely on the ledge, on the other side, with plenty of room to spare.

Snakey looked back and saw that Tamba had not caught up to them yet. He had an idea. "Stop," he hissed. "What?" asked Bear as he skidded to a stop?

"Take me back over to the right, close to the edge, near the tree bridge." Snakey instructed him.

Bear quickly responded and they reached the bridge.

Snakey then uncoiled from Bear's neck and dropped to the ground. He said, "You go five or six steps to the rattle side, and act like you can't find me."

Bear obeyed.

Tamba arrived at the gorge and stopped to survey the situation. He saw Bear looking around helplessly and bumping into things.

The snake flopped around on the ground, appearing to be injured.

Tamba growled and stepped forward onto the tree bridge. He was careful and cautious as he balanced on the tree. He began to drool as he neared the middle of the bridge.

Suddenly Snakey coiled up and looked quite healthy and full of fight. Snakey had no problem moving as he darted out onto the bridge to face Tamba.

Because of his precarious position, Tamba could not raise his paws to defend himself. Snakey struck at his nose and made contact. Tamba screamed in pain and tried to back up, but almost lost his balance. Snakey moved closer and struck again, sinking his fangs a second time into Tamba's nose. Once again, Tamba screamed in anger and pain.

Chapter Fifteen

"Take that, you big bully. You thought you'd make a meal of me, huh?" Snakey yelled at Tamba, then coiled for one more strike. Tamba began backing up fast, too fast. His back legs slipped off the tree and he tumbled off the bridge, screaming as he plummeted down into the gorge.

Snakey called after him, "See you around, you big boob!" He peered over the edge of the tree bridge in time to see Tamba land with a splash in the water far below.

"What happened?" asked Bear.

Snakey replied, "When he was coming across the bridge, I attacked and bit him. Then he fell off the tree into the gorge. He was totally defenseless, the big dodo."

A confused look crept over Bear's face. "Bear thought you couldn't crawl. How did you..." "I've healed, I'm okay now," Snakey replied.

"Okay," said Bear. ----After a silence, he asked, "Will you be leaving now?"

"Actually," Snakey responded. "I thought we had an agreement. We'd stay together until we were both healed."

A look of surprise and joy swept over Bear. "Bear didn't think you would..."

"What? Do you think Snakey could desert you now? I do have my honor," said the snake as he moved closer to Bear. "Now bend down your big head so I can climb back on."

Bear lowered his head and Snakey coiled himself back around the enormous neck. Bear then began walking down the trail.

Chapter Sixteen
The Celebration

In the Kiltook Village, a grand celebration was taking place. Great racks of whale meat were drying, oil extracted, and portions given out to each villager. Seemi appeared at the edge of the common area and grimly stumbled into the crowd. He forced a smile and waved. "Thank you," he said, mistakenly thinking the celebration was in his honor. "I've completed my walkabout," he stated.

Chief Sagawan saw Seemi and beckoned him to approach, then said, "Welcome back Seemi, You must eat." The chief handed Seemi a large portion of meat.

Seemi took the food and bowed. "I didn't expect such a big celebration for my return," Seemi mumbled.

"It is not for you. Today, I Chief Sagawan, with the help of Spirit Singer, our Circle of Feathers, hunted and killed a mighty whale."

Seemi realized his mistake and backed away from the chief. "Oh, I thought…"

Chapter Sixteen

Chief Sagawan said, "Tomorrow our visitors will be leaving. They should wish to make a purchase that involves you. I have already given my blessing, but you must complete the agreement. Seemi was visibly flattered, saying, "Thank you Chief Sagawan for your confidence." Seemi then took his ration of food and walked away. He gobbled it quickly as he walked, oil dripping down his chin. He stumbled to the entrance of Spirit Singer's lodge and went inside.

The next morning No Face went to wake Seemi and found him passed out on his sleeping mat, still wearing his dirty tattered clothes from the day before. No Face shook Seemi and said, "You must wake up."

Seemi opened one eye still feeling very groggy, and said irritably, "Can't you see I'm sleeping? What is it?"

No Face replied, "Chief Sagawan and Spirit Singer want you at the beach."

Seemi sat up and wiped his eyes. Slowly he came awake and stood up to stretch, then said, "I remember now. The chief wants me to assist in conducting negotiations with the traders." No Face helped Seemi out of his dirty clothes, pulling his tattered shirt over his head.

Seemi began bragging, saying, "I completed my walk-about in the forest. I am now a man, and I will be treated as a man."

No Face helped pull the clean shirt over Seemi's head and then helped him into clean garments as Seemi continued bragging,

The Legend of Elos Mountain

"Someday, I will wear the circle of Feathers, and your master will be one of the most powerful men in the tribe." Seemi smiled proudly at No Face and added, "Don't worry No face. I'll still keep you around."

Seemi's statement troubled No Face, but he quickly dismissed the thought.

Spirit Singer entered the lodge and saw Seemi still dressing and said sternly, "The chief is waiting for you. Come now!"

Seemi started to put on an ornamental necklace and Spirit Singer slapped it out of his hand and said,

"Your vanity, put it aside just this once."

Spirit Singer's action startled Seemi.

The shaman pushed the boy out the door and they walked quickly toward the beach with No Face trailing slightly behind.

Spirit Singer spoke quietly, "You must complete an agreement – that is what Chief Sagawan wants of you." "Forget the grand thoughts that dance in your head," said Spirit Singer. "A purchase, that is what the traders wish. A trade is what you must complete."

Seemi was puzzled and asked, "What is this trade all about?" "This you will find out about soon enough," answered Spirit Singer.

At the beach, the Mayukett traders had their canoes ready. Azart was talking with Chief Sagawan when Spirit Singer, Seemi, and No Face arrived.

Spirit Singer introduced his nephew to Azart, "This is Seemi, my nephew. He is the owner of the property in question.

Chapter Sixteen

Seemi faces the Mayukett.

Seemi was more confused than ever as Spirit Singer turned to him and said, "These are the Mayukett people. To trade with the Kiltook people, that is why they have come to our shores."

Seemi nodded as Azart stepped forward, carrying a box.

"I am Azart of the Mayukett people. I wish to trade for your slave No face."

Seemi glanced at the chief who nodded his approval. He said, "but…"

Spirit Singer raised his hand and silenced the boy.

Azart walked up to Seemi, carrying the wooden box under his arm, saying, "We the Mayukett people, to show our thanks to you Seemi, for finding and taking care of our brother White Bear, son of Dancing Rain. To honor you, we give you this mask of power."

Seemi took the mask and examined it, but to him it was just a stupid old mask. He looked at No Face who was all smiles. It was a slap in the face. They wanted to take away his slave. He suddenly pushed the mask back at Azart, saying. "This isn't enough." Azart refused to accept the mask and it fell to the sand. "I want more than that useless mask," cried Seemi. Seemi's rejection and poor manners angered Azart. He stepped around Seemi, grabbed No Face by the arm, and began leading him to the canoe.

Seemi ran after Azart, grabbed No Face, and began pulling him back. A brief tug-of-war ensued until Azart stepped forward and shoved Seemi.

Seemi lost his balance and fell to the sand.

Spirit Singer hurried to restrain Seemi. However, before he could get there, Seemi drew his knife and lunged forward.

Azart pushed No Face into the canoe, and turned to deflect Seemi's attack. The two struggled over the knife, twisting their arms and thrusting the knife at one another.

Spirit Singer tried to break up the fight by breaking Seemi's grip, as the knife suddenly darted down and then up. Seemi felt the knife sink home. Azart let go of the knife and stepped back. Seemi, still clutching the weapon, looked in horror as Spirit Singer doubled over and fell backward. As he fell, the knife pulled free from his chest. Spirit Singer's blood spilled onto the sand.

Seemi stood in shock, blood coating the blade of his knife.

Azart stumbled back and started for his canoe.

Spirit Singer's blood spilled onto the sand.

Chapter Sixteen

No Face watched in horror as Seemi ran up behind Azart and stabbed him in the back. Azart fell over the edge of the canoe, and looked up at No Face with stunned glassy eyes.

The remaining Mayukett reached for their spears to defend themselves.

Chief Sagawan drew his knife and many of the Kiltook elders and other warriors drew their weapons. The Kiltook group quickly charged and attacked the Mayukett in their canoes, wounding several of them. The rest put down their weapons and surrendered.

The elders dragged No Face out of the canoe onto the beach.

As they passed the spot where Spirit Singer lay dead, he saw Seemi kneeling down next to his fallen uncle and weeping openly. Seemi looked at No Face. He gritted his teeth and glared. He shouted, "This is entirely your fault! You will die! You will die!" Hysterical, Seemi collapsed over his dead uncle's body.

Later the same day, the tribal council met in the chief's lodge.

Chief Sagawan sat on the raised platform with his family at his side.

The senior elders gathered around the carved wooden statue of the Great Bear. Four Kiltook guards tied No Face and the other prisoners together in one corner of the lodge.

Seemi held the talking stick and spoke to the congregation from the center of the lodge. "I was attacked. I fought back, but the Mayukett killed our great shaman, Spirit Singer, who I will miss very much. They should all be put to death."

A murmur traveled through the elders and Chief Sagawan leaned closer to one of the elders to confer. After a few moments, Chief Sagawan raised his hand to stop the discussion. He turned to Seemi and said, "Blood has been spilled, both of Kiltook and of Mayukett. Our great Circle of Feathers, Spirit Singer is dead. But, so too is Azart, the leader of the Mayukett traders."

Morning Star looked at No Face, as a tiny ray of hope swept across her face. Chief Sagawan continued, "I do not believe the Mayukett came here to attack our people. It was a misunderstanding. Seemi frowned, anticipating the ruling. "So my decision is that the Mayukett will become slaves to the household of the Tyee elders; one slave per household of the most senior elders. And you Seemi, your slave No Face shall continue in your service."

No Face was stunned. Chief Sagawan stood and motioned to Seemi, saying, "Seemi, come forward."

Seemi was apprehensive, but he followed the chief's orders and stepped up to the platform. He bowed. One of the senior elders indicated that he should get down on his knees. Chief Sagawan reached into a small box he was holding and lifted out the Circle of Feathers. The feathers appeared stained with Spirit singer's blood. Chief Sagawan held the Circle of Feathers high in the air. Drums began beating and the elders began chanting. Morning Star was sickened by the spectacle. No Face cringed and put his hands over his ears. He could not stand listening to the sounds. At a signal from the chief, the drumming stopped.

Chief Sagawan spoke, "As Spirit Singer's nephew, and as Kiltook tradition requires, you, Seemi, should wear the Circle of Feathers for the Kiltook people. To honor your claim to the hereditary rank of shaman to the Kiltook people, and to honor the memory of Spirit Singer, the tribe will hold a Potlatch. Seemi, as our new Circle of Feathers will host the celebration. Our finest artisans will raise a Totem to honor the occasion. May the Great Spirit honor you and protect our people." The chief placed the Circle of Feathers around Seemi's neck. Seemi then stood and backed away from the platform. The drumming began again and the elders lined up to congratulate Seemi.

Chapter Sixteen

For many weeks prior to the Potlatch, members of Seemi's clan were busy creating appropriate gifts. There were rattles and boxes with intricate carving, finely woven leggings, blankets and dance aprons. The new mortuary pole stood 20 feet tall with a replica of Spirit Singer and a miniature canoe to hold the shaman's remains. At the very top of the totem, an eagle spread its wings in flight. The day of the great celebration finally arrived and the entire tribe gathered in the common area. They listened to stories and songs that told of all that Spirit Singer had accomplished during his life, as well as dramas that kept the history of the tribe alive. No Face had to swallow his misery and serve food to all the guests, as well as wait on his master.

Chapter Seventeen
Arrival of the First Snowfall

Deep in the forest, snowflakes began to float down through the trees and onto the ground.

Bear sniffed a few flakes up his nose and sneezed.

"Bless you," said Snakey. "Winter is coming.

It is time for Bear and Snakey to sleep," replied Bear.

"Perhaps we should go back to the cave we found," Snakey suggested.

Bear nodded in agreement, then turned and walked in the direction of the cave. As the companions reached the cave entrance, Bear spoke, "You know Snakey, Bear just wants to say thank you. You are very brave, and a good friend for sticking with Bear."

"You're not going to get all mushy on me are you?" Snakey quipped to cover his embarrassment.

"Bear is serious. Bear has always been alone and done everything for himself. However, the fire changed everything. When Bear needed your help you came through."

"Oh right, so now we're going to kiss, is that it?" said Snakey.

Snakey should stop joking," he said.

"Okay," replied the snake.

"Bear is proud to know you Snakey."

Snakey accepted the compliment and then said, "I'm proud to know you too, Bear."

"See you next Spring," said Bear.

See your next year," Snakey added as they settled in front of the Cave Bear.

"Yah, see you next Spring," said Bear."

"I bet you will," said Snakey. "Your eyes will surely be healed by then."

"Bear did as the Cave Bear asked. When life returns to the forest, Bear will be able to see again. Yes, perhaps by spring." He concluded, then closed his milky-white eyes and fell asleep. Snakey relaxed his hold on Bear and dropped to the floor of the cave. He looked at the bones of the cave bear, yawned, and then fell asleep.

As both began their hibernation, the cave walls began to change. They became transparent windows that revealed scenes of snow covered mountains, glaciers, blizzards and cold wind.

Back in the Kiltook village, huge banks of snow engulfed the lodges. It was a cold windy day with low dark clouds that emptied an endless shower of snow onto the world below.

No Face shivered with cold as he tried to separate some wood from a frozen pile. Grabbing a few sticks, he trudged through the snow back to the lodge entrance. Inside Seemi's lodge, it was warm and cozy. No Face opened the door and stumbled as he went through the doorway, allowing the door to swing wide, letting a gust of snow swirl inside.

Seemi glared at No Face and yelled, "Close that door you fool! You're letting all the cold air in."

No Face added the wood he had brought to a stack next to the fire that was burning in the center of the lodge. The boy then lingered around the fire trying to get warm.

Seemi asked, "Is it really cold out there, No Face?"

No Face, his spirit broken, turned mindlessly in the direction of the voice and answered, "Yes, it's really cold."

"Good," Seemi answered. "I have a long list of chores I want you to finish outside.

No Face turned and walked over to where Seemi was sitting. He stood, waiting for his orders.

Seemi was looking through some of the containers that held Spirit Singer's herbs and magic potions. Seemi said,

Chapter Seventeen

"I need some bark from a maple tree for the Welcoming of Winter ritual I'm to perform this evening."

As Seemi continued searching through the containers, No Face worked up the courage to ask a question. "Since you are now Circle of Feathers, do you have new powers?"

"Yes I have many new powers," Seemi answered.

"Perhaps you could ask the clouds to stop the snow," No Face suggested.

Seemi looked up at No Face and smiled mischievously, "I could, but I won't."

A wry smile crossed No Face's lips.

"Oh, you think it's funny? See if you think it is funny a few hours from now. I'm going to need bark from the birch, the fir, the aspen and the oak as well as the maple," Seemi continued. "I'll need at least five armloads of each. I'll need them all by sunset, so get to work."

No Face opened the door and held it wide for a moment. Outside it had stopped snowing, the wind had died down, and the sun had cracked through the clouds. No Face made sure Seemi could see the weather, before exiting and closing the door.

Later in the evening, inside the chief's lodge, a group of women danced around the fire in the center of the room. There was drumming and singing. The women wore costumes that included themes of wind, snow and ice.

Seemi fed pieces of bark into the fire, holding each one in the air and mumbling a blessing before tossing it into the flames. The new shaman picked up a small bundle of colored cloth and stepped away from the fire and up near the platform where Chief Sagawan and his family sat. The drumming stopped and Seemi held the colored cloth into the air. Then he spoke, "With these prayer ties, I send homage to the Spirit of the sacred mountain, to the Spirit of the North, and the Spirit of Winter." Seemi unraveled a string of cloth from the prayer tie and handed it to Chief Sagawan. Seemi then stepped back and untied a group of strings, which he handed one-by-one to the elders. Seemi held a single string of his own. He pulled the one string so that all of the strings separated and formed a shape like the five radial arms of a starfish. Seemi continued his prayer, "Oh Great Spirit, I ask for your blessing. I ask you to protect us through the winter. To keep us warm, to keep us fed, and to keep us alive. Seemi then began walking with his end of the prayer tie, weaving his cloth string over and under the others. The string tangled, forcing Seemi to step over a tangled mass, which tripped him and sent him sprawling onto the floor.

There was laughter from the spectators in the lodge, however, Chief Sagawan raised his hand and there was silence.

Seemi sat nervously trying to untie the knots that surrounded him.

Seeing that it was going to be a long process, Chief Sagawan stood and motioned to Seemi, saying, "That is good Seemi. We will eat now." The drumming resumed and the women started serving platters of food. Chief Sagawan looked down at Seemi and motioned for him to join the chief's party on the platform. The chief said, "Eat with me tonight, Circle of Feathers."

Seemi wadded up the remaining tie cloth and haphazardly tossed it into the fire.

The gesture raised eyebrows among the elders.

Seemi totally missed the sign of disapproval, as he proudly took a seat next to the chief.

Chapter Seventeen

No Face brought platters of food to the platform. He put one of the platters near Morning Star. She looked at him and smiled with sympathy.

As they ate, Seemi eyed Morning Star intentionally.

She saw that he was staring at her, and looked away to avoid his glance. Each time she checked to see if he was still staring at her, he was.

Finally, Seemi turned to the chief and spoke, "Chief Sagawan. May I speak with you about a matter regarding my status as Circle of Feathers?"

The chief nodded and said, "You may speak with me."

Seemi said, "Since I am now a man, and have been given the title of Circle of Feathers for the Kiltook people, I would like permission to take a wife.

Chief Sagawan turned and studied Seemi for a moment. He then slowly nodded his approval, saying, "What you say should be the truth. You are a man now and you should have a wife if you want one. Is there someone in particular, or should I choose a wife for you?"

"Your daughter Morning Star," was the answer.

The chief turned to Morning Star, who was shocked at what she heard. The chief studied his daughter, who averted her eyes and stopped eating. After a pause, chief Sagawan said, "Morning Star would have been my choice as well. She is headstrong and sometimes speaks out of turn, but I'm sure you will discipline her and teach her what her proper place is." The chief then raised his hand and the drumming stopped.

No Face turned to see the chief stand to make an announcement, saying, "When the summer comes, and we move our village to the Elos Mountain camp, our Circle of Feathers will take my daughter Morning Star as his wife.

No Face dropped the dirty platters he was carrying. He quickly picked them up as the drumming continued and the tribe began to yell and cheer.

Morning Star could not look at anyone. When some of the women came to congratulate her, she did not respond.

In the giant cavern, high up on Elos Mountain, Bear and Snakey were deep in their winter hibernation. The rapid eye movements under Bear's eyelids revealed that he was in the middle of a long dream.

Chapter Seventeen

A small pool of water in a corner of the cave began to boil from geothermal radiant heat. Steam began to fill the air. The gaseous cloud thickened to the point that the sleeping Bear appeared to be floating inside a cloud of mist. Inside the cloud, the shadow of the cave bear appeared. He glided over to the sleeping bear and snake and bent down next to them. An opening appeared in the mist and the Cave Bear looked out to see that the cloud floated above the Kiltook village. Looking down at the village, the Cave Bear saw the people suffering through the harsh winter.

Inside Seemi's lodge, the fire had gone out. Seemi woke shivering and tried to get the fire going again, but did not have any luck. He walked over to the sleeping No Face and kicked him awake. He shouted, "Wake up you good for nothing. You let the fire go out."

No Face tried blowing the coals back to life.

No Face got up and went to the fire. He put fresh wood on the coals and tried blowing the coals back to life. There was a sudden knock at the door.

Seemi went to the door and opened it. A group of Tyee elders were huddled together in the snow. Along with Chief Sagawan, they entered Seemi's lodge.

The chief spoke, "All of our fires have gone out and none can be relit. You are our Circle of Feathers. You must do something. Use your power now, or we will all perish from the cold."

Seemi panicked. He turned back to his own dead fire trying desperately to get the fire restarted, while mumbling incoherent incantations.

As the cave bear looked down at the village, the clouds moved and obscured the view. He looked back at the sleeping bear and snake who were with him inside the cloud. The clouds parted again, and this time the cave bear saw the people in their lodges crowded together trying to find warmth.

Everyone huddled in groups, eating cold food. They ate hungrily, including Chief Sagawan.

Morning Star had no appetite. She did not eat.

In the Circle of Feather's lodge, Seemi was eating some cold food.

No Face sat alone in the corner. He was not eating.

After a few minutes, Seemi's complexion changed to a sickly green. He became pale and sweaty. Suddenly he scrambled for a waste pot and began to vomit. While his head was still in the waste bucket, there was a knock at the door.

No Face went to the door and opened it to reveal Morning Star.

She came into the lodge and said. "Everyone is sick. The food has all gone bad and my father is very ill. He wants the Circle of Feathers to do something. He must do something now." No Face pointed to Seemi as he retched into the waste container by his pallet.

Chapter Seventeen

The Cave Bear, once again alone.

The clouds again obscured the village and the cave bear was once again alone with the sleeping bear and snake inside the cloud. There was a great movement in the clouds. Darker shadows appeared and swirled. Flashes of lightening sliced through the blackness of the dark clouds. An opening appeared and the cave bear looked down as a tremendous rainstorm pelted the village below. A thousand leaks poured from holes in the roof of the chief's lodge. They used every available container to catch the water. The great thunderstorm blasted sheets of rain-whipped wind at the village. Men sat in the rain on the roofs of their lodges, trying to hold the planks in place. They placed rocks in position, but still the wind flipped the boards up and let the water pour inside.

The Legend of Elos Mountain

In the burned-out forest, water poured over the ashes, eroding great troughs of mud. The muddy tributaries joined other larger mud streams traveling down the mountainside.

The villagers were caught by surprise.

In the Kiltook village there was loud roaring sound as the massive river of mud came churning down the mountain. It emptied into the village and buried three of the lodges nearest the beach. The mud then poured into Elos Bay changing its dark blue color to muddy brown.

The clouds once again obscured the cave bear's view. He looked back down at the sleeping bear and snake. A ray of sunshine illuminated the cloud. The cave bear looked up at the light. An intense beam shined in a small circle around him and the two sleeping companions. The radiant heat warmed and comforted them as they slept. The cave bear looked down out of the clouds at the earth below. The beam of light was moving over the burned part of the forest. As the rays passed over an area, the forest was instantly renewed. Flowers sprang forth, plants of all types grew, and insects appeared. Trees sprouted and unfolded their branches. New life burst into existence everywhere.

The Shaman's Lodge

Meanwhile back in the shaman's lodge, Seemi was sleeping, clutching the Circle of Feathers as he snored. No Face crept past his sleeping master and moved to open the door. He quietly exited the lodge. No Face walked quietly to the next lodge, opened the door quietly, and eased his way silently inside. He searched until he found his fellow Mayukett slave, sleeping in the corner. No Face woke him and they quietly talked in whispers. They agreed that they and the other slaves must find the right time to steal canoes and escape.

Chapter Eighteen
Seemi performs the Rite of Spring

An early Spring.

Spring came early to Elos Mountain that year. Seemi was excited. He stood in the center of the common area performing a ritual for a rag tag collection of onlookers. "I thank you Great Spirit for the spring." Seemi prayed. "And I thank you for helping us through the hard winter. I thank you for giving me the strength and power to overcome the evil spirits that besieged us.

Several of the villagers walked away in disgust. Seemi continued sprinkling cornmeal in a circle and shaking the rattle.

No Face watched as Seemi made a fool of himself in front of everyone in attendance. When Seemi finished the ritual, he went immediately to No Face and bragged. "I have the respect of the entire tribe. They look up to me as their great spiritual leader.

No Face could not believe Seemi's boastful attitude, saying, "The people are tired of winter. They suffered greatly.

Many of them blame the Great Spirit for their troubles. Many even blame you."

"Blame me?" he said in disbelief.

"You are the Circle of Feathers," No Face explained. "You are supposed to deliver the people from evil and use your powers to protect them."

Seemi shook his head and laughed. Then he said, "You really don't get it, do you?"

No Face looked at Seemi in astonishment.

"I made all those things happen." Seemi said proudly.

"Why would you do such a thing?" No Face asked.

"So Chief Sagawan would move the village immediately."

No Face shook his head in amazement and said, "I see. You did it for your own selfish reasons."

"Yes," answered Seemi. "And you know what?"

"Yes, unfortunately, I think I do."

"It worked," said Seemi. "We're moving the village in two days. So, get to the lodge and start packing everything. Within the week, we will be at the Elos Mountain camp and I will wed Morning Star.

No Face grimaced when he heard that news.

Seemi then turned and prepared to leave, saying, "I have some important arrangements to make with Chief Sagawan. I'll meet you later in the lodge to see how well you've followed my instructions." No Face watched Seemi walk away towards the chief's lodge.

No Face then hurried off in another direction. He saw two of the other Mayukett slaves doing chores outside one of the lodges. He stopped and told them the tribe was moving in two days. He said, "Tell the others we have to make our escape before the camp moves to its summer camp." The two slaves listened to his message and nodded their agreement.

The Legend of Elos Mountain

Bear had a strange dream in the cavern, Bear slowly awoke from his long hibernation. As he stirred, something tickled his nose.

Bear twitched in irritation.

Snakey had obviously been awake for a while. He had moved a few inches in front of Bear's face. He flicked out his tongue to tickle Bear's nose.

Bear opened his eyes. His eyes were still milky white.

"I thought you'd never wake up." Said Snakey.

"Is it spring?" asked Bear.

"Hey, it might be summer for all I know. Can you sleep or what?"

Bear stirred and stretched.

Snakey looked at him in anticipation and asked, "Well? How are those eyes?"

Bear looked around. "It's dark, Bear can't see anything."

"I forgot about my night vision and all, and its pitch black in here," said Snakey. "I'm sure when we get outside; you'll be able to see again."

Bear leaned his head down and Snakey crawled back into his position around Bear's neck. "bear had a strange dream," the grizzly confided.

"Me too," said Snakey.

"We were in the clouds," said Bear.

Snakey responded, "Yeah. I dreamed about clouds too."

"Bear saw terrible things happen to the human village."

Chapter Eighteen

"I saw those things too. What were you doing in my dream?"

"Bear doesn't think it was a dream. Bear thinks it was a vision."

"On no," said Snakey, "That's not good."

"We need to do something," Bear replied.

Snakey sighed and said, "That's what I was afraid of."

"We need to go to the human village and help them," Bear insisted. "The boy who helped us against Tamba lives there."

"Oh yeah," replied Snake, "I'm sure that's exactly what they need…A huge ten-foot grizzly with a snake wrapped around his neck. Uh huh. That's going to go over real big."

Bear started walking toward the cave entrance, where he began digging his way out of the hole. Finally, he stood on the surface in the bright sunlight.

Snakey bent his head around to peer into Bear's eyes. He flicked his tongue in front of Bear's eyes. The eyelids blinked, but his eyeballs were still milky white.

Snakey started to say something about Bear's eyes, but changed his mind and said, "Hey, you know, we've been down in that cave a long time. I bet you've worked up a monstrous appetite."

"Yeah, Bear is mighty hungry," was the reply.

Snakey noticed the blackberries growing all around them. He looked at Bear and said, "There are berries everywhere. Why don't you fill up, while I take a few minutes to shed my skin?"

Bear bent his head down and Snakey slithered off. Bear then sniffed and began eating large mouthfuls of berries. He used his paws to pull the vines close, and then used his lips like fingers, plucking the berries into his mouth.

Snakey went through his ritualistic wiggling to shed his old skin, peeling it back like a glove, one inch at a time.

Snakey wiggling to shed his skin.

On the bluff overlooking the village, No Face sat on the edge, peering down at the village below. As he sat, he heard someone approach. He turned to see Morning Star who looked around cautiously, as No Face stood to greet her.

Morning Star said, "One of the Mayukett slaves said I should come here to talk with you."

"Yes," replied No Face. Thank you for coming. It's very hard being unable to even speak to you."

Morning Star spoke with impatience, "What is it? What do you want?"

"I want you, I need you," was his reply.

"You know that is not possible. I shouldn't even be here. If anyone saw us," she lamented.

No Face cut her off. "Don't worry," he said. "No one will see us. I just wanted to tell you something."

Morning Star looked away, dreading his words.

"We are escaping tonight. All of the Mayukett," said No Face.

Chapter Eighteen

Morning Star stared at him in shocked amazement. "You can't do that. They will kill you. Can't you understand?" she pleaded.

"We must go. We have to try, and we must do it before the village is moved to the mountain," he stated with great urgency in his voice.

Morning Star was visibly upset at his words, "Why can't you just stay with us?" she asked, "Why do you have to go and risk your life like this? Tell me why."

"I can no longer bear to be a slave. My place is with my people, either in this world, or the next," he stated firmly. "If you were a slave in the village of my people, you would feel the same burning in your heart, to be free. You know it's true."

A tear welled up in Morning Star's eye. She asked, "So did you get me here just to tell me goodbye?"

"No," he replied. "I want you to hear my final plea to come with me on this journey. You fill my heart and I need you by my side." Whether we make it to my people or not, we should be together. Your vision showed you that quite plainly. It led you directly to me."

"I can't go with you," she replied.

"So don't think of the things that bind you to his world," he said urgently. "We are going to a new place, a new world, where a bear and a deer can live together."

She answered with pain in her voice, "But I am to marry Seemi, the Circle of Feathers. My father says it is my destiny."

"Is that truly what you want?" he asked.

Morning Star paused, and then she looked at No Face and began to cry. "No it's not," she answered through her tears.

"Then consider my plea." He begged.

"I just don't know," she sobbed. "I'm afraid. I can't decide what to do.

No Face gently touched her chin, lifting her face so they were staring eye-to-eye. "Tonight, a bear will come to the rear of your lodge. If he finds a deer there, they will go together. If he does not, he will go alone, with a very heavy heart."

They looked longingly at each other, and then Morning Star turned and hurried back to the village.

Some time later, No Face quietly entered Seemi's lodge. He took some powders and roots from Seemi's medicine box and put them into a small leather pouch. As he worked, he looked up cautiously to make sure no one was around.

Suddenly, Seemi entered the lodge and saw No Face working around the supplies.

No Face acted as if he was cleaning up and preparing to pack the supplies into traveling baskets.

"It's about time you cleaned up and began the packing, slave. I've been way too lenient with you."

"As soon as I've finished cleaning, I'll get everything packed." No Face replied.

Seemi glowered at his slave and said, "Well, at this rate, you'll be up all night."

"Don't worry," said No Face. "When you wake up tomorrow, everything will be taken care of."

"Well, just be quiet while you work. We have a long journey tomorrow and I need my rest," Seemi ordered.

Chapter Eighteen

No Face continued cleaning. It was twilight when one of the Mayukett slaves carried a platter of food down to the beach. He stopped and emptied the powders from a small pouch into the food. He then continued to the canoes where two scouts guarded the beach. The scouts pulled the platter of food from his hands. They quickly devoured the meal.

Bear and Snakey were moving along through the dense undergrowth of the forest. The sunset was beautiful, and Snakey admired it. He looked again at Bear's eyes, disappointed by Bear's inability to see the intense beauty of the waning light.

Bear stopped when he smelled something interesting.

"What is it," asked Snakey.

"Juicy tubers, Bear is still hungry," was the answer.

Snakey responded, "Boy, you sure can eat."

Bear dug for the food and located several tasty roots. He then began to eat.

"At this rate," said Snakey. "We'll get there is a week or so. I'm sure whatever it is we need to do, can wait."

"Bear needs food for energy. Need energy to walk," said Bear as he continued to eat.

"Okay, if we're taking a break," said Snake. "Let me down so I can find something to eat myself. I haven't eaten in months."

Bear leaned his head down and the snake crawled off into the brush, hunting for a meal.

Back in the Circle of Feather's lodge, Seemi was sleeping as No Face crept past his master, carrying a small bundle with his belongings.

The Legend of Elos Mountain

Seemi stirred and rolled over.

No Face froze and waited for everything to settle back down. He then continued walking very slowly to the door. Once he was outside Seemi's lodge, No Face crept around to the rear of Chief Sagawan's lodge. He waited in the tall grass at the edge of the village. There was no sign of Morning Star. No Face continued to wait, as the stars slowly moved across the sky. Then in the darkness, No Face heard a sound. He looked around, but saw no one. When he turned to look behind him, he was startled to see Morning Star. She had crept up behind him. The two leaned closer and let their lips come together. They kissed passionately.

Seemi stumbled from his lodge and walked in a sleepy daze behind the structure. He untied his lower garment and began to relieve himself in the tall grass.

Behind the chief's lodge, Morning Star and No Face broke their embrace.

"We must go now," said No Face. The two turned and began walking softly through the grass.

Seemi heard something as he stood behind his lodge. He looked around cautiously, as a troubled look crossed his face. He saw something out of the corner of his eye. He turned his head and was shocked to see a deer. The deer looked at Seemi, then turned and ran past him into the center of the village.

Having finished, Seemi retied his garment and hurried to the front of his lodge, looking for the deer. It was running toward the beach. Seemi quickly entered his lodge to get his bow and arrow. Seemi returned with his weapon and ran in the direction of the water. He reached the beach and looked for the deer. He hid in some brush and slowly crept forward, then jumped out onto the sand, hoping to surprise his prey. Instead, he found the beach deserted. He was puzzled and turned back towards the village. As he walked

away, he nonchalantly looked out at the dark water of Elos
Bay. He saw two canoes, just disappearing from sight,
moving along the coast. Seemi realized that something was
wrong. He once again turned and ran towards the village.

Farther up the coast, No Face and Morning Star were
paddling together inside one of the two canoes. The remaining Mayukett traders were scattered between them. As No
Face paddled, he saw great jagged rocks that jutted out of the
water. The waves crashed into the rocks creating permanent
white foam that glowed in the darkness. The moon silhou-
etted the two canoes as they made their run north, along the
coastline. After paddling intensely for a time, the paddlers
stopped to rest.

One of the Mayukett saw a light in the distance. It was
coming towards them. Despite all their efforts, the light was
growing brighter. It was a torch.

Seemi and his warriors in the war canoe.

"It's them," cried Morning Star. "They're coming after
us. They're coming!"

No Face responded, "We can't outrun a war canoe. We
have to find a place to hide." They continued paddling with
all their strength. No Face searched the beach looking for a

place to hide. He watched as a small narrow inlet appeared in the cliffs. "There! Go in there," No Face directed.

The two canoes turned and sped into the inlet. As they passed through the narrow entrance, they entered very still water. They paddled along looking up at the tall canyon walls. Both canoes pulled in behind a row of boulders that jutted out into the waterway. There they hid and waited. Soon they heard the sound of voices, and watched as a large Kiltook battle canoe cruised past the mouth of the inlet. A man holding a torch stood in the bow. Immediately behind, a second battle canoe slithered across the front of the inlet.

No Face leaned towards the second Mayukett canoe and whispered, "We should wait a bit longer, then paddle out to the open ocean.

Suddenly, one of the Kiltook battle canoes appeared at the mouth of the inlet. It turned and headed straight for the fugitives, who could not escape. The huge canoe blocked their escape route. The canoe's full complement of warriors were armed with bows and arrows, all aimed at No Face and his people. Standing in the front of the canoe, holding a torch, was Seemi.

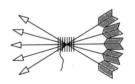

Chapter Nineteen
The Death Sentence

The entire village assembled in the common area in front of the chief's lodge. The slaves were tied securely, ankles and wrists bound. The chief and the elders sat together in judgment. Morning Star and the rest of the chief's family sat at his side. Seemi sat next to the chief.

Chief Sagawan stood and motioned for Seemi to stand with him. The chief then turned and addressed the village. "My thanks go to you, Circle of Feathers." You saved my daughter Morning Star, who was stolen from us by our enemies."

No Face looked at Morning Star, but she could not look at him. She was silent. When she felt his glance, she turned her head away.

Chief Sagawan continued, "I have showed great mercy to these people. This is what we have received in return. Since the Mayukett have lived with this tribe, we have had nothing but bad spirits. The spirits of Elos Mountain are angry, just as we are angry."

Seemi looked at No Face and beamed with satisfaction as the chief gave his final judgment saying. "We will offer our enemies as a sacrifice to the spirits of Elos Mountain. We will take them with us to the mountain camp. When we arrive, we will cleanse our mountain village with their blood. And following the sacrifice, we shall join together our Circle of Feathers with my daughter Morning Star." Morning Star closed her eyes to fight back the tears.

In the forest above the Kiltook village, Bear and Snakey reached a clearing near the edge of the village. Bear slowed and crept carefully towards the outskirts of the common area. As they looked around, they realized the village was deserted and only the main lodge pole supports for the lodges remained. All the support planks, walls, and roofs were missing. Nothing remained but a smoldering fire in the center of the village.

Bear shook his great head and said, "Bear is too late. They are gone." Snakey looked around and commented, "I'd say gone for sure."

"Lodges and everything – gone," said Bear.

Snakey leaned out from Bear's neck and looked at Bear's eyes. They were no longer milky white moons. They had returned to normal. Snakey said, "Hey Bear, You can see!"

Bear looked around and blinked his eyes, "Yes, Bear can see. My eyesight is restored like the Cave Bear promised."

Snakey leaned way out, looked at Bear and asked, "Can you see me?"

Bear answered, "Yes, you are scary." Bear shuddered and shook Snakey off onto the ground. "So that's the thanks I get," said Snakey as he coiled up and raised his head in indignation. Then he hissed, "Is that the way you treat your friends?"

Bear looked down apologetically and said, "Sorry, Snakey. You scared Bear. You are really ugly."

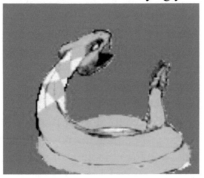

Chapter Nineteen

"Well, rub it in why don't you," the snake replied. "And I guess you think You're beautiful, with your patchwork hide and those big clumping feet. Then there is that terrible breath."

Bear responded sheepishly, "Is it that bad?"

"Hey, I was going to say something," Snakey answered, "But I thought gee, the guys been asleep for months. He's going to have a really bad case of morning breath."

"Bear is sorry," the grizzly said looking down.

Snakey flicked out his tongue and said with a sigh, "I guess this is it then."

"It?" said Bear confused.

"This is where we part ways," Snakey stated.

"Snakey will leave Bear?"

"Hey," the snake replied, "This is where this adventure started for me and it looks like a good place to get off."

Bear was silent, but he nodded his head in understanding, and then said, "Bear will miss Snakey."

"Great!" Snakey replied. "Now you get sentimental on me. That's just what I need, is a 1,200-pound grizzly crying on my shoulder."

Bear ignored the sarcasm, saying, "Thank you, Snakey. Thank you for helping Bear. I know you have a right to leave, but there is one last thing Bear must do and Snake deserves to be a part of helping the boy who helped us both."

Snakey soaked in the complement and then turned and prepared to leave. He moved a few feet and then stopped and turned back, saying, "Hey Bear, you're right. The human deserves our thanks before we say goodbye."

Bear lowered his mighty head and Snakey slid snuggly around Bears neck once more. Bear sniffed the earth around the lodges. He then slowly followed his nose up to a trail that led out of the village and up the side of Elos Mountain.

On the forest trail, well up the side of the mountain, the Kiltook people were on the move, walking in a seemingly endless line, up the forest trail. They carried all of their belongings, including the building materials for their lodges. The prisoners were carrying the lodge support poles, and cross members, sweat pouring from their bodies under the strain.

No Face looked around to see if he could find Morning Star. He did not see her anywhere.

Chapter Twenty
The Wedding and the Execution

The first elements of the tribe arrived in the open area of their spring camp. The main frames of their lodges were standing where they had left them the year before. The winter had left some damage and the villagers began making the necessary repairs. More people arrived and began constructing their lodges.

No Face and the other Mayukett lay tied together. Kiltook warriors stood guard over them.

Soon after nightfall, the Kiltook people assembled before a great fire that burned in the center of the mountain village. A rhythmic drumbeat throbbed with deep bass emotion.

Chief Sagawan walked from his lodge with Seemi and Morning Star to a circle of stones. There he tied their wrists together, binding them firmly.

No Face and each of the prisoners lay tied to one of the large meat drying frames. Each prisoner, spread eagled on a drying rack.

Chief Sagawan raised his hand and the drumming stopped. With the sudden silence, Morning Star looked up with great apprehension. She saw her father nod to Seemi.

Seemi, proudly wearing the Circle of Feathers, spoke. "Great Spirit, accept this sacrifice and protect our people. Cleanse our village from evil spirits, and bless my union with Morning Star."

Seemi began his ritual prayer.

Chief Sagawan looked to one of the guards near the prisoners and nodded his head.

Four guards lifted the meat drying rack that held the struggling No Face. He pulled at the ropes that bound his hands and feet, but was helpless.

The warriors carried the wood frame to the fire. They then stopped and waited, looking for the next command.

Morning Star began sobbing uncontrollably, "No, No, No."

Chief Sagawan gave his final nod and the drumming started again.

As the men carrying No Face, prepared to pitch him into the fire, Morning Star began pleading with her father. "Please, don't do it father! I beg you! They did not take me. They did not! I left of my own free will. It was my choice!" Morning Star pulled at the wrist binding that connected her to Seemi. She struggled to reach her father.

Chief Sagawan looked very sternly at his daughter, and waved his hand boldly for the execution to begin. Morning Star fell to her knees, dragging Seemi down with her.

Seemi tried to pull her back to her feet.

Chapter Twenty

After struggling for a moment, Morning Star looked back at No Face and screamed. "Ahhhhhiii!"

As Seemi looked down, attempting to quiet her, Morning Star continued screaming, her arm slowly rose as she pointed.

Seemi looked up just as several other villagers began to scream.

It was Tamba running full speed at Seemi.

A great black roaring monster appeared. It was Tamba, running at full speed straight toward Seemi.

Tamba swatted one of the executioners into the fire. The warrior's clothing caught on fire, but he was able to escape the flames.

The other men dropped the frame holding No Face. They ran away in different directions.

No Face looked up to see Tamba coming straight for him.

Tamba ran to the frame holding No Face, his tremendous paws missed the boy by inches, but he smashed and splintered the wood frame.

No Face was able to free one hand. He used his free hand to work the other bindings loose.

Tamba seemed preoccupied with anything that moved. He began randomly attacking people in the crowd. As he swatted one victim out of his way, he suddenly saw Seemi running for safety with Morning Star still tied to his wrist.

Seemi pulled out his knife and began slashing at the wrist bond, trying to free himself from Morning Star. The knife caught Tamba's eye and he leapt forward, straight toward Seemi.

Seeing the crazed bear charging, Seemi slashed blindly through the bonds, cutting Morning Star in the process. With blood running down her arm, Seemi pushed Morning Star into Tamba's path.

At the sight of Seemi's cowardly act, the crowd, including Chief Sagawan, gave a gasp of anger.

Tamba stopped and looked down at the helpless girl. He smelled the blood. His mouth watered as he bared his teeth, and gave a tremendous scream.

Morning Star did not try to run. She stared directly at her attacker as Tamba swung back his mighty forepaw, extending his claws and prepared to strike her. Morning Star closed her eyes as the massive paw swung toward her head.

Before Tamba could make contact with the girl, Bear hit him broadside and knocked Tamba off his feet.

He landed ten feet away and rolled to a stop. He looked up enraged. He was shocked to see Bear, his massive body standing to his full ten feet. Around his neck, Snakey moved his head back and forth menacingly. Regaining his equilibrium, Tamba charged, but Bear met him head on, knocking Tamba back with a vicious series of blows, tearing great wounds in Tamba's body.

Snakey managed to make contact with Tamba's neck, injecting his venom into the already wounded bear. Bear continued his relentless onslaught, backing Tamba to the edge of a rocky precipice, where Tamba's rage and momentum caused the ledge to collapse, throwing Tamba into the deep canyon below. Bear turned back and faced the Kiltook people.

Bear gave a mighty roar.

Bear stood to his full height, and then raised his head to the sky, with Snakey waving his own head in victory; Bear gave a tremendous roar that vibrated through the entire camp.

Chief Sagawan looked in amazement to see No Face standing beside Bear, wearing his mask of the grizzly bear with white moon-eyes.

No Face raised his arms in victory.

Seemi looked out from his hiding place, cowering.

Morning Star cried, a mixture of joy and amazement.

A great roar of anger erupted as the tribe reacted to having witnessed Seemi's cowardly act. He had slashed Morning Star's arm in his despicable attempt to save his own life.

There was consternation at the site of the giant grizzly nuzzling No Face.

The council members around Chief Sagawan called for the chief to take vengeance on Seemi. Others called out for him to restore freedom to No Face and the other Mayukett warriors.

Morning Star stood riveted as Bear and Snakey turned to one side and trotted off into the forest, leaving No Face gazing out over the Kiltook people who had so recently wished him dead.

Chapter Twenty

That night Chief Sagawan called the tribal elders to his lodge and made a grave pronouncement. "The Great Spirit has shown us that Seemi, Spirit Singer's nephew, is not fit to wear the sacred Circle of Feathers. The elder discussed the matter and everyone agreed. Chief Sagawan said, "Each clan will provide seven warriors to form a gauntlet of shame, through which Seemi must pass as he is expelled from the tribe."

The next morning there was a solemn ceremony at the camp. Chief Sagawan stood before the tribe with No Face and Seemi. The chief removed the Circle of Feathers from Seemi's neck and said, "You, Seemi, are no longer a member of the Kiltook people. The council has spoken. You must run the gauntlet of shame and leave the tribe, never to return."

Seemi bowed his head and slunk away in disgrace. The crowd formed a gauntlet and turned on Seemi with sticks, fists and feet. He fell beneath the blows, but managed to get up. With tears streaming down his face Seemi got to the end of the line. He ran into the forest and did not look back.

Chief Sagawan then turned to No Face. He held out the Circle of Feathers and said, "All I have, I offer to you White Bear. Tell me what you want and it will be so."

No Face responded, "I was just a boy when I was washed up on this shore. Instead of being treated with the kindness due any child who has lost everything dear, I was enslaved and misused. On the other hand, I am thankful for the kindness of Spirit Singer and for the love of Morning Star who has tried many times to speak up in my behalf. You asked what it is that I want. First, I want to take Morning Star as my wife. Then I wish that my bride and I, along with the other members of the Mayukett party be allowed to return to our own people.

Chief Sagawan called for an elder to place the ceremonial wrist thong on No Face and Morning Star. The elders all gathered around, as well as the entire gathering, who all

The Legend of Elos Mountain

wanted to witness the union of No Face and Morning Star. Chief Sagawan kept the ceremony simple and brief, giving his blessing to them both and ending with the final words, "you White Bear and Morning Star are now and forever more, man and wife."

No Face, Morning Star and the Kayukett traders on their journey home.

The following day, No Face walked to the edge of Elos Bay and pushed off the first of the two canoes carrying his Mayukett brothers. No Face turned and looked back and smiled at Morning Star, who rode behind him. From high atop Elos Mountain, the smoke from a mighty campfire floated into the air and joined what appeared to be a mighty curling snake that looked out over the ocean, far below, as two small canoes moved off into the distance.

The End

Made in the USA
Columbia, SC
21 July 2024